J

HARRIET TUBMAN

Freedom's Trailblazer

Illustrated by Robert Brown

HARRIET TUBMAN

Freedom's Trailblazer

by Kathleen Kudlinski

ALADDIN PAPERBACKS

New York   London   Toronto   Sydney   Singapore

First Aladdin Paperbacks edition January 2002
Text copyright © 2002 by Kathleen Kudlinski
Illustrations copyright © 2002 by Robert Brown

Aladdin Paperbacks
An imprint of Simon & Schuster Children's Publishing Division
1230 Avenue of the Americas
New York, NY 10020

The text of this book was set in New Caledonia.
Designed by Lisa Vega
Printed and bound in the United States of America

2 4 6 8 10 9 7 5 3

Library of Congress Catalog Card Number:2001095514

ISBN 0-689-84866-8

ILLUSTRATIONS

CONTENTS

The following have provided assistance and inspiration:

Kay McElvey, EdD, and the staff at the Harriet Tubman Organization, Cambridge, Maryland; Pauline Copes Johnston, Alice Norris, the Reverend Paul G. Carter, the African Methodist Episcopal–Zion church, and the Harriet Tubman Home in Auburn, New York;
The Reverend Michael Bolduc, U.C.C.

Scars

"You mean to tell me you're five years old? A scrawny little thing like you?"

Minty stared at the floor, confused by the white woman's questions. *Mama!* she wanted to call out, but Mama was nowhere in this big, strange house. And the man who owned her family, the man who had named her, Master Brodas, had whipped up his horse to pull the wagon down the road without ever even looking back. *Mama is not coming,* Minty told herself. *Not ever.* Her eyes filled with tears.

"Never you mind," Miss Susan said briskly.

"I paid good money to hire out a slave to help with the baby. Mr. Brodas said you could do the work." She sniffed. "And so you will."

Miss Susan shifted her child off her wide hip and handed him to Minty. "Hold him while I change for dinner." The child squalled and wiggled in Minty's arms. "If you drop my little Charles Lee," the woman said, smiling sweetly at the baby, "I'll whip the skin right off you, girl." Then she turned and walked out of the room.

Minty's arms went weak. "Mama!" her lips moved, but no sound could come out. Not now. Not after that.

The baby twisted to watch his mother's long, squash-colored skirts swirl then vanish through the door. Minty struggled to keep her balance. Charles reached his fat arms toward the door, and Minty almost dropped him. None of the babies in the slave cabins was this fleshy! She sat down so she could hold him tight in her lap.

"Oh!" she gasped. The floor felt soft through Minty's thin cotton shift. She rubbed her bare feet on fabric as fuzzy as a bumblebee's backside. The baby giggled with the movement. Minty glanced at the edge of the floor and blinked. It wasn't made of packed dirt at all, but wooden boards, cut flat and melted together somehow. She stared.

Charles whimpered. "Hush-a-baby," she tried to calm him. "Y'all be good, now, you hear?" The baby looked up at her. The air was so hot that her black skin and his white were stuck together with summer sweat, but when she looked into those sky-colored eyes, she shivered. Charles looked about to cry, so Minty kept talking. "Hush, pretty baby." She made her voice soft and happy-sounding. "This child here, she don' want a whipping," she babbled, "nohow, I don't. No, sir. No, sir." She pictured her older brother's back, bruised and bleeding after a lashing. Then she thought about her father's back, crisscrossed with old scars. She remembered the sound of her sister, screaming in pain. Then she made herself stop thinking.

Suddenly the baby's fat little hand was pushing at her lips. He was trying to stick his pink finger into her mouth! "What you want, baby?" she asked. Charles smiled. "You like my talking?" Now he grinned, showing little baby teeth as white as his soft gown. "I can sing for you, too, I reckon." The baby waved his arms. "Oh, Go down, Moses," Minty sang. "Way down in Egypt's land, . . ." She began rocking in time with the church hymn. "Tell old Pharaoh, 'Let my people go.'" The child lay quiet on her lap. Minty smiled. *I can do fine here,* Minty thought, starting the next verse. *I jus' got to sing, and*—she swallowed hard—*and never, never drop this here baby.*

"Give him here, Araminta." The sound of her new mistress's voice made Minty jump. Was it dinnertime already? Her stomach growled, and she struggled to her feet, handing Charles to his mother.

"Wait outside, girl," Miss Susan said. "When the meal is done we'll feed you and the dogs." Shocked, Minty hurried toward the door. "Not that one!" the tone in Miss Susan's voice put a chill down her neck. "Use the servants' door, back behind the brooms and buckets." There were two doors in this house? Slave cabins had only one, and no windows, either. Minty scurried through room after room, toward the back of the house. She didn't have to ask what would happen if she used the wrong door.

The floor under her feet had soft cloth on it. Minty couldn't help it. She slowed down to shuffle across the strange smoothness. There were clothes on everything. She looked into a room. The table had a dress on it. The windows wore dresses, too, with ruffles. Minty smiled. Little tables wore scarves with fringe. The chairs were dressed in fuzzy, colored cloth.

5

Minty wanted to rub her hands on all of it.

The walls were as flat as the floor, and all dressed in stripes and roses. And the ceiling? She stopped in wonder. The ceiling was as white as Miss Susan! Where did the cooking smoke go? Minty sniffed. The air was empty. No friendly smell of food cooking on the fire. No smell of family bodies all together and sweaty. No smell of wood from log cabin walls. No smell of home at all. Just the breeze off the ocean, scented with salt and the sharp tang of low tide in the marshes. A gull cried, lonely in the distance.

"Get out, girl!" Miss Susan stamped her foot against the wood floor. Minty jumped and ran. The white woman's laughter chased her out of the house.

"Now, Minty." Miss Susan stood in the lamplight next to the bed. She stretched her arms wide and yawned. Minty stared. No one she knew had so many teeth. And no one wore a pretty dress to bed. This one was pale pink, with tiny flowers stitched around the edges. "My sister is coming tomorrow," Miss Susan said. "I need my rest tonight." Minty looked down at the baby lying on a soft pink pillow in a cradle beside the bed. "Keep Charles quiet, so I can sleep."

Miss Susan blew the lantern out, lay down on the bed, and pulled snowy white sheets over her dress.

Minty sat down beside the baby and began singing to him.

"Quiet," Miss Susan growled in the darkness over her head.

Minty hummed as quietly as she could.

"Hush your mouth!" Miss Susan scolded. "Girl, I've got a switch up here, and you know I'll use it."

Minty blinked back tears and reached her hand out to rock the little cradle. At home, Mama would be saying night prayers over everyone resting on the floor. Papa would say a verse from the Bible to sleep on, and the day would be done. Minty said a prayer now, but silently. Soon the only sounds were Miss Susan's snores. Starlight washed in through the glass of the windows, softening the shadows in the room. Minty yawned and settled against the wall, her hand still pushing the cradle, back and forth, again and again.

"Wanh!" Charles's cry woke Minty just before the lash whistled down toward her head.

"Ow!" she cried, startled by the sound, the moonlight in the room, and the sudden pain along the back of her neck. "Ouch!" she cried as the switch fell on her again.

"You stupid pickaninny!" Miss Susan's voice was as sharp as the pain itself. "Rock the baby!"

Rock, rock, rock, Minty's hand moved the cradle. Little Charles hiccuped himself back to sleep again. Miss Susan's snores were louder now. *Mama!* Minty wanted to cry.

Mama! She felt a trickle dripping down her neck, but kept rocking the cradle. The moon was staring at her full in the face through the window. She yawned. *Stay awake*, she scolded herself. *But how?* Minty sang in her head all the church songs she knew, rocking the cradle in time to the music that only she heard. Then she sang all the songs again. She didn't remember losing her place before she jerked awake again at Charles's groggy whimper.

"Thwack!" The lash fell, harder this time.

"Sorry, miss, sorry," Minty begged, but the lash silenced even this.

The moon moved past the window, and darkness filled the bedroom again. Presently the faintest dawn woke a distant rooster. The stars winked out, one by one, beyond the glass. Minty's head was nodding when Miss Susan finally sat up and stretched. "Get up, you lazy thing," she said. "It's time to get to work."

Pig Freedom

"How dare you just sit there!" Minty jumped to her feet at Miss Susan's angry voice.

"I don' know what else to do, miss." The last bite of cold breakfast biscuit turned to dust in Minty's mouth.

"Don't you know anything, girl? The house must be perfect for Miss Ellen's visit. Get yourself a broom and a dust cloth and make that parlor room shine!"

The parlor? Minty shuffled her feet against the brightly patterned carpet as she wandered down the front hall. *What is a parlor?* She peeked into a room full of shelves. From floor to ceiling, rows of colored bricks stood edge to edge. Minty wandered into the room. One of the bricks lay open on a table. It was a Bible! The minister looked at one almost like it when he said verses on Sunday. The white people held them, too, when they sang from the pews down in front of the church. Minty stared at the shelves. *So many Bibles!* She couldn't count near that high. *Miss Susan is a wonderful good Christian.*

"Girl!" Minty dashed out, following her mistress's voice into yet another room. "Sweep!" a broom was thrust at her. "And dust." The dust cloth flew through the air at her head. Minty grabbed the broom and swept wildly as Miss Susan left. Dust filled the air. It sparkled all around her in the sunshine from the windows. Minty laughed aloud and whirled in a circle, dancing with the dust stars, until she saw the switch. A

long willow branch was lying on a shelf over the fireplace. Suddenly Minty swept harder. Coughing, she leaned the broom against the door and grabbed the dust cloth.

When she was done, the wooden chairs and tables gleamed, even under their lacy white aprons. The keys on the piano were spotless. Every little seashell, every glass doll, and every little framed picture had been moved, dusted, and returned to its place. Minty looked around the room, took a deep breath, and skipped back to the kitchen.

"Minty!" A screech brought her running back to the parlor. "Didn't I tell you to sweep and dust?" Minty raised her arms to protect her face as Miss Susan thrashed at her head with the willow stick. At last her mistress paused for a breath.

Minty looked around. Dust dulled every surface.

"But, I . . . ," she started.

Miss Susan drew a line in the dust on top of the piano with her finger. "Do it again, you stupid little darky!" Her voice was cold with anger.

Minty cried as she swept the floor this time. She didn't dance with the dust. Her face and neck stung. Her ear was bleeding, too, where the willow switch had sliced an edge. Finally the parlor was done.

"Get yourself in here!" Minty could hardly make her legs move down the hallway again. Three times she'd cleaned the room the best she could. Three times she'd been beaten for it. "You call this clean?" The stick whipped down on her head as she slunk through the parlor door.

"No, miss, don't!" Minty sobbed. She twisted and bent, trying to hide from the beating.

"What are you doing to the child?" A stranger in a blue dress stood in the doorway. Minty tried to cover her head, as the lash fell again. "Stop at once, sister!"

"She's wasted the entire morning playing in here, Ellen," Miss Susan said, trying to reach Minty around her sister's wide skirts.

"Stop, I tell you!" Miss Ellen's voice was firm and calm.

"She's a willful little thing," Miss Susan said. "Only the lash will tame her."

"Why, she's just knee-high to a milk pail," Miss Ellen put her hand right on Minty's head. "Mayhap she doesn't know any better."

Miss Susan snorted.

"Girl," Ellen went on, "have you ever done housework before?"

Minty looked down, sniffling and hiccuping back her sobs.

"I thought not."

Minty watched Miss Susan's skirts swirl as she stamped out the door.

"Try this," Miss Ellen told her, "sweep first. Wait a bit until the dust settles back down. Then come use the dust rag." Minty nodded.

It made sense. She glared around the parlor, hating every table and picture, chair, and piano key. *Three more days—and nights— and I can see my mama,* she thought.

"Amen!" Mama called out at church the next Sunday. Minty nestled in beside her mother's bulk on the bench. Her sisters sat behind them in the women's section. Papa sat across the aisle with the men and all of Minty's brothers. Twelve children, four benches. Minty always loved having everyone near in church, back from all the farms where Master Brodas had hired them out. This Sunday was even sweeter. Mama's arm curled around her as the minister's voice rang out.

"Remember when Moses had to leave behind his people in Egypt, all of them slaves?" The black section in the back of the church grew still, listening. The minister glanced out the window. So did the slaves. Everybody knew that the sheriff was out there, listening, in case the minister said something to make the slaves expect to be freed.

"Moses broke a law and killed a man. He ran to escape. He ran all the way to Midian. People were good to him there. He had a wife and a son. He was free. But was he happy?" The minister paused. "No," he answered for everyone. "No, he wasn't. Moses missed his people. He said, 'I have been a stranger in a strange land.'"

After a week at Miss Susan's, Minty knew how it felt to be away from home. She nestled closer to her mama. "But the Lord had something to say to our Moses," the minister's voice rose. "He came to Moses in a vision. A bush flamed with a white-hot fire right before Moses' eyes, but that bush did not burn up." The minister waited for that to sink in. "And God spoke to Moses right out of the fiery bush. He told Moses he was sending him to lead his people out of Egypt. Out of slavery."

The church was deathly quiet now. "Well, brothers and sisters," the minister went on, "Moses didn't believe it was the Lord talking. So God sent him more signs and visions and told him what would happen in the future. And finally Moses believed."

He dropped his voice. "And so the lesson for ya'll today—" No one in the white section seemed to breathe. The sheriff leaned in through the open window and stared at the minister. "The message is, be ready for the Lord." The whites relaxed in their pews. "The God of ancient Moses is here today, in eighteen twenty-five, talking to you, right here in Cambridge, Maryland."

Minty blinked. *Here? God?* She looked around.

"Listen for His voice," the minister said. "Watch always."

Minty sat up straight. *Watch? For what? A burning bush?* She tried to imagine God speaking to her, Araminta Ross. To a slave. It wasn't possible, she knew, but she couldn't help thinking. *It would be so wonderful!*

Soon the whites were in the front of the church taking the sacrament, drinking wine and eating bread. Minty's stomach growled. It had been a long time since breakfast. Mama's hand closed over hers and gave it a squeeze. They sang a hymn, then listened some more.

By the end of the service, Mama's arm was resting heavily on Minty's sore neck. Minty shifted to move it. Mama lifted the hair from Minty's shoulders and made an angry mother hen sound. Minty's sisters Linah and Sophie leaned forward to blow on her neck from their pew. The breeze felt good as love on the hurt places.

Later, as the slaves and free blacks followed the white churchgoers out of the Methodist church, Minty got a scolding. "You listen to me," her mother said. "You got to take care of yourself, some. You got to fight back."

Minty thought of the willow switches ready in every room of Miss Susan's house. "How, Mama?"

"You gots to be clever, but act simple. Remember Anansi?"

Minty grinned. Everyone knew the trickster stories about sly old Anansi. Slaves had brought the tales with them from Africa. They were told and retold around fires, at bedtimes, and even during long walks. Whether Anansi was a spider or a man in the stories, they always made Minty laugh.

"Well, honey child," Mama went on, "nobody ever knew how that Anansi was going to trick them, but he always be makin' plans."

In the weeks that followed, Minty acted simple during devotions at Miss Susan's house. While the family's prayers were loud, Minty's were silent. In secret, she was asking

God to make her strong and able to fight. She pretended to like napping under the kitchen table with the dogs. She didn't talk much anymore, either, but she did watch everything and make plans. She saw that Miss Susan was extra cranky in the mornings. That was when she reached for the switch most often. So Minty began putting on extra layers of clothes to start each day. That way, the lashings didn't hurt so much. She made sure to scream just as loud, though, when she got hit. Miss Susan did not seem to know the difference. As the day went on and her mistress's mood got better, Minty took off the sweaters. Now, when Miss Susan called her a "stupid little pickaninny," Minty smiled—but she was careful not to let the smile show on the outside.

Minty learned how to stay awake all night, too. It made the days seem very long. Soon she didn't have to pretend so hard to look stupid. She was so tired, it was hard to think at all. One day when Miss Susan hit her, Minty yelled right back at her. This time the beating was so bad, Minty thought she was going to be killed. She had to get away!

That afternoon Miss Susan handed her an armful of dirty diaper rags to empty into the outhouse. For once, Minty didn't mind the stink. She carried the slimy pile to the outhouse door, grabbed a last breath of fresh air, and ducked inside. Her job was to unfold the rags and drop their contents into the hole, then bring the diapers back to wash. Minty just threw the whole mess down the pit and ran toward the woods.

She finally gasped a lungful of air behind the summer kitchen house. The air held the sweet smell of yams roasting, dinner rolls baking, and ham frying, too. Minty's mouth watered, but she kept running. She ducked under the low-spreading branches of a holly tree and leaped over a fallen log. The shade was thick beneath the pines, but the forest was only a wide strip between farms. Minty threaded her way between tree trunks until she was almost out into the next field. There was more light here, and the briars grew thick. She curled up on a patch of soft ferns. Her ribs on that side hurt, so she turned over. Then she shifted again. It didn't matter which way she lay down. There were bruises everywhere. At least she was free of Miss Susan and her temper.

I did it, she thought, looking through the ferns. *No one knows where I am.* At a scuffling sound behind her, Minty froze. *This child is in for it now.* She knew her next whipping would be even worse. She lay, hardly breathing, while the rustling moved closer to her head. Moments later a fox squirrel crept into view, big as a cat. He stared at her, silvery whiskers quivering, then bent to dig at the dead leaves.

She watched him sit back on his haunches and nibble a toadstool. Next he ate a grub, then a shiny black beetle. *You're big enough to make a stew for the whole family,* Minty thought. She breathed again. She could almost smell Mama's squirrel stew, bubbling away in the old pot on the cook fire in the middle of their cabin. Minty blinked back tears. The squirrel barked at her and dashed away.

Without him, the woods seemed empty. Her bruises hurt. The mosquitoes bit her face, and a jay began scolding from a branch far overhead. "She be here," he seemed to shriek. "She be here!" *It's hopeless. I can't get away, nohow.* Minty curled into a tighter ball and cried herself to sleep.

It was dark when her stomach grumbled with hunger. She shook herself awake and looked up. Stars twinkled at her through the trees. *I'm free!* Minty thought. She remembered Miss Susan's face, twisted with rage. *I ain't never going back,* Minty decided. Her stomach growled again, and a stick cracked loudly in the dark woods behind her. *What is there?* Minty tried to see in the starlight. *Could be a wildcat? Or a rattlesnake? Or worse.* Minty thought about the stories of ghosts and spirits haunting the night. *Please be a wildcat!* She pushed herself to her feet and scrambled through the brambles toward the safety of the farm.

Halfway there, she stumbled in a water-filled ditch. She lay half in, half out of the slimy water and sniffed the air. *Food?* Her stomach tightened. Mixed in with the smell of barn and pigsty, she could tell there were dinner scraps nearby. She made her way to the pigpen. There, slopped over the edge of the trough, ham scraps and yam skins, bread crusts and apple peelings lay scattered in the starlight.

Minty ate as much as she could, then slept again. Most of the next day she slept, too, hiding in the tall rushes in the ditch. When she heard Miss Susan calling her, Minty settled lower into the water and stayed there.

When Cook came out with the bucket of slops for the pigs that evening, she didn't miss the trough. Minty could only stare through the fence as the animals grunted and squealed, pushing their snouts deep into the food. Her stomach grumbled. Minty reached her hand through the fence poles. She could almost reach the trough. She reached farther. Her hand was in, among the pig's heads. She grabbed a handful just as the old sow grunted a warning. Minty pulled her arm back, fast as lightning. She knew what pig's teeth looked like. The sky was cloudy, so she had to sniff to tell what was in her hand. It was only crusts of burned corn bread and a crumbly piece of crab cake.

Minty ate every bit and licked her fingers. She shivered in the night wind. The cold spread through her, but at least there was no Miss Susan sleeping next to her. No cranky baby. No whip.

It was her cough that gave her away. Exhausted, half starved, and bone-chilled, she had come down with bronchitis. The cook had heard her coughing and carried her back to the house. Miss Susan sent her back to Mr. Brodas. "I wouldn't give you a copper half-cent for this no-account nigger!" she said. "She's stupid and willful, besides."

Mr. Brodas slapped Minty's head as she fell over into the wagon. "What you got to say to Miss Susan?" Minty knew he wanted her apology. She didn't speak. She couldn't. Her throat was on fire, and her chest burned, too. Minty didn't care. At last she could go home to Mama.

A Child No Longer

"Baby girl, come in the light and let me look at you." Mama stood next to the door. Minty pressed her dress flat with her hands and stood tall in the late afternoon sun. "You be growing up," Mama said. "Seems 'bout ten years since old Brodas named you."

"You be fixin' to give her Linah's head cloth?" Henry asked. Minty stared at her older brother. "'Bout time, I reckon." Minty's breath stopped. Grown women always wore a cloth over their hair. Not little girls. A smile spread all over inside her.

But wear her sister's scarf? The smile died before it reached her face. It had been two years, but Minty could still hear Linah's screams and the horrible clanking chains as she and Sophie were led away by the slaver. Then they were gone. Minty thought of them often. Were they still in chains? Were they dusting some parlor somewhere? Worse, were they dying in the heat of rice or sugar fields way down South? Minty blinked back tears as she felt Mama tie the head cloth at the back of her neck.

"Linah always help me with the babies," Mama said, her voice quivering. "Your looks favor her some."

Minty raised her hands to feel the precious cloth on her head. "I won' let them sell me South, Mama," she promised. "I be here, taking care of you always." Her voice was as raspy raw as it had been since she'd run from Miss Susan.

Mama's sobs filled the little cabin.

"Now, Rit." Minty's father put an arm around Mama. "It's Saturday night. Weedin' is done, and clothes are out to dry. Try and put your mind on dancin', now."

"Rit?" the call came in through the door. "Ben? Shake a leg, y'all!" Mama took a shuddering sigh and wiped her eyes. Minty grabbed her hand and led her outdoors. They joined the long line of Brodas's slaves snaking through the woods toward the sound of drums.

"Where'd your hair go, Minty?" The shopkeeper's boy fell into step behind her.

"A place you never see!" she teased back, stomping her feet in time with the drums. She'd never paid much attention to her neighbor before. *He is free,* she realized. She'd always known his daddy had saved up and bought himself from his owner. That meant his son was free, too! *A free man is walkin' me to the carryings-on!* She tossed her kerchiefed head and made her skirt swish with each step.

They gathered as the sun set, sharing a supper around a cook fire in the woods. Blankets were spread over the grass. Plates of possum, slow-cooked with sweet potatoes, lay next to hog jowls and greens. A bowl of hominy flavored with bacon drippings sat near by. Chitterlings, baked grits, sweet corn—there seemed to be no end to the fine food. After Minty ate her fill, she watched the younger children, all brown and naked, chasing the fireflies in the field. Her niece Mary Ann caught the first one and handed it to an even younger child. Minty smiled at their games. Then she took her place among the adults by the fire.

"Another runaway lit out from the Greene place," someone announced in the darkness near her.

"God be with him," she heard. And, "There be friends along the way." Minty knew that slaves shared hiding spaces with runaways. Free blacks offered food and shelter, too.

She'd even heard that a few whites helped out, here and there.

"Hush your voices," Daddy whispered. "Old Greene won't know Joseph's missing till Monday field call"—he looked around the circle slowly—"less'n he hears it from one of us."

"He'll be branded if he's caught." Firelight flickered on the R-shaped scar on the speaker's cheek. "Or have half his foot cut off so he can't run ever again." Warnings came from around the fire: "Some runaways are whipped raw and salted down." "I saw someone with a cage of bells locked over they head. Rang day and night. They couldn't never sneak off again. Couldn't sleep, neither."

"Joseph be lucky to live through the beating he's goin' get," a deep voice offered. "Prob'bly be sold South," someone else said, "where there's no hope."

Minty shivered, wishing she could still play with the fireflies.

"What do you think, Ben?"

Minty felt proud that they were asking her own daddy.

"Don't know much 'bout runnin'," he said, his voice slow and low. "But I purely do love dancin'!" He jumped to his feet. A drum started, and the folks stood and stretched, laughing as they chose partners. Bones rattled in time, and a mouth harp twanged. Minty got up and smiled as the free boy came across the grass toward her. The dancing went on for hours. Circle dances made them all change partners. Everybody made up their own fancy steps to show off on their way to the pies and cakes. Some of the dances came direct from Africa. Others were invented on the spot.

Mama began telling stories to the children. The dancing broke off as people stopped to listen to the old tales. Hare and Anansi played their clever tricks. Bible stories came to life, too, by the campfire. Visions and miracles, tricksters and family stories followed one after another. Children cuddled together nearby like puppies in the grass. At first they listened. Soon they all were fast asleep. Minty was wide awake. Since those night whippings at Miss Susan's house, she never did sleep much. The adults settled in to singing, low and soft into the night. Finally they picked up their buckets and their babies and headed back to their cabins at farms scattered around the dark countryside.

"Think on it." Terrance wiped sweat out of his eyes. "We could be house slaves, under a roof in dry clothes."

"Not me!" Minty called back low across the field. "I wan' be where I can see the sky." She thought about how trapped she was in that parlor with Miss Susan and her whip. Minty felt the old flash of anger. It made her strong. She raised her hoe and slammed it into the soft Maryland dirt. "Jus' feel that air!" She held her face toward the north. The wind blew free across the flat land, whipping clouds and gulls along as it went. "I could live outdoors," she boasted.

"A good thing, too," the overseer said. "I hear tell nobody in Charlestown will have you in their house." He shook his whip at her. "Nobody be wantin' you a'tall if I has to beat you senseless for talkin' in the daytime."

Minty ducked her head and grinned. She drove her hoe into another weed, jerked it out in a spray of sandy soil, and moved on down the row of tomato plants. At the end of the row she turned and worked back toward the barns, picking big green caterpillars off the plants. Some she squeezed, some she squashed under her bare heel, others she hurled into the ditch.

"You miss one," the overseer reminded her, "and you eat it." That didn't scare Minty. Brodas had been renting her out to farmers for years. She'd never seen anybody forced to

eat a tomato worm. But she had seen them use their whips plenty.

Minty's back creaked as she turned to head down the next row. She stretched and looked at the overseer. He was glaring at her, so she gave him her stupidest look and tried to plan some trick. Practice made her quick. Like greased lightning, her hand darted toward the nearest tomato plant. She pretended to grab a worm and stuff it right into her mouth. Smiling at the overseer, she pretended to chew. The overseer closed his eyes and looked away.

The slaves in the field nearby nodded at her. They didn't stop their work, though. Instead, one started a call. Minty responded, echoing his tune with her strong, husky voice. The other slaves joined in, calling and answering. The chanting went on long into the afternoon about Moses leading the Israelite slaves free of the pharaoh in old Egypt. They sang the hymn, "Amazing

Grace." They sang about Joshua knocking down the walls of Jericho with a blow of his horn. The overseer stood in the shade of a tree, fanning his face with his hat.

Minty glanced at him. Who was stupid, here? she wondered. In their songs, the slaves were also talking about a neighbor who had run away from his owner a month ago. One chant signaled that he had gotten across the river safely. "I once was lost, but now I'm found" meant he'd made it out of the slave states all the way to Pennsylvania. Slavery was against the law there, so he was free as soon as he crossed the line. You could be a slave right here in Maryland or next door in Delaware, but free right across the border into Pennsylvania. *Free*. Minty closed her eyes with pleasure at the thought. And now her old neighbor had sent word back, friend to friend, field to field.

All the while overseers everywhere fanned their stupid faces in the shade of the trees.

* * * *

"Psssst, Minty." The whisper floated to her on the winter wind one day in 1835. She pulled at old, dry cornstalks. Later they would be used to feed the Bucktown Store owner's cows. Today they had to be yanked from the frost-hardened dirt and heaved across the rows. She bent to pull out another.

"Harriet," she hissed back at the tall boy working nearby. "I not be 'Minty' no more. I be 'Harriet' now." It had felt good to give herself a name of her own. Fifteen years of hearing the ugly "Araminta" day and night was enough. *That name belonged to Brodas, not to me!* She jerked another stalk up so hard, she had to take a step backward for balance.

"Will y'all listen a minute!" The whisper sounded so full of trouble that Harriet almost stopped in her work. "I's going," he said. "Now."

Harriet stopped.

Think, she scolded herself. *Plan.* In two

heartbeats she picked up the work rhythm again. If her friend was going to run for freedom from the shopkeeper's field, he needed to go without warning. If the overseer knew, he could, by rights, kill him. She glanced at their guard. He was looking at the two of them. Harriet swallowed. The cold wind was freezing her fingertips through the rags she'd wrapped about her hands. Fear chilled her much deeper.

"God be with you." She prayed softly so her friend could hear. "Send word when you are clear."

"Come along?"

Harriet squeezed her eyes shut. "Can't. Mama and Daddy needs me here."

"Word is"—the boy bent to pull a fallen corn shuck—"old Brodas is sick. Any day he could sell them." He tossed the withered plant. "Or you."

"No talking, you!" the overseer barked at them. He cracked his whip in warning. "Go to the north edge of the field, boy. You, girl, stay put."

Harriet made herself look away as her friend shuffled toward the edge of the field. "Hey!"

She forced herself not to look when the overseer's whip cracked again, then again.

Help him, Lord, Harriet prayed.

"Stop, y'all!" the overseer roared. Still, Harriet kept her eyes down on the ground. She made her face stay blank, though her heart was soaring. She knew the others around her would be doing the same. Their boredom might confuse their guard. And this way, they couldn't be blamed if the boy escaped. If he made it. Harriet could almost feel the field humming with hopeful prayers.

The boy's footsteps thudded across the dirt road and pounded up the wooden stairs of the little Bucktown Store. The door squeaked open and banged shut. "Hey!" the shopkeeper's angry voice floated across the field. "No! Stop!"

What was happening? Did her friend mean to hide in the store? To steal food? To kill before he fled? *I've got to know,* Harriet thought, trembling with curiosity. *Besides,* she thought quickly, *I have reason to go. I'm hired out to the shopkeeper. I can pretend to help.* Suddenly she was leaping over the fallen corn shucks, flying across the road, jumping onto the porch. She threw the door open and froze.

"Stop him, Harriet!" her owner shouted.

Harriet's friend leaped from behind the counter and ran toward the door. Toward her. Things seemed to be moving slowly. The shopkeeper reached his hand down to the counter and picked up a weight from the scale. He pulled his arm back, taking aim. "Stop him, Harriet!" he repeated.

Harriet opened her mouth to say "no" and watched her owner hurl the weight. Her friend pushed past just as the weight hit her head. She heard the metal sound of it hitting; heard the crunch of her own skull bones crumpling. She felt herself twist and stagger backward out the door.

Her face was wet. The world was red, but she blinked and pawed the blood from her eyes. She had to see. *Did he get away? Did he?*

Her foot slipped off the edge of the porch, and she fell backward into blackness.

Prayers and Visions

"Minty, baby?" Mama Ross knelt beside her daughter on the floor of the slave cabin. "Harriet?" she pleaded. "Come back to us." She used a wet rag to wipe the flies away from the awful wound on Harriet's head. "Dear God," Mama said, rocking back and forth, praying, "spare this child."

"Ma-Mama?" Harriet thought she heard her mother's voice far in the distance. She sounded so sad. Harriet fought to get to her, to help her, but the fog was too thick.

✻ ✻ ✻ ✻

"It's been weeks." A new voice floated in the mist. Was that Master Brodas? "She'll never make it, Ben. Give her up for dead."

"No!" Ben's roar filled the cabin.

Harriet tried to call out, "Daddy." She made the word in her mind, but her tongue wouldn't move to make the sound. She struggled to shake the word free, but something held her head down. A pain. A terrible, burning pain. It was easier to sleep.

Harriet blinked. The sun was so bright in her eyes. She felt air spilling across the floor from the door. It was warm on her cheek. But it was wintertime! "Mama?"

"Oh! Praise the Lord!" Harriet heard the voices clearly. "Send for Rit. Get Ben, too. Minty is back!" Footsteps thundered by her poor, sore head.

"I'm here, baby." It was Mama's voice. Harriet struggled to focus her eyes. A ring of heads were around her now. She blinked.

They were her brothers and sisters!

"Mama?" she called. And then Mama was there, big and strong, spooning something warm into her mouth.

"Hat, baby. We were so afraid." Harriet swallowed as much as she could, then closed her eyes. "She's tired, y'all. Can't you see? Now, clear the room." More footsteps. "Baby, pray with me," Mama said, "then sleep. Our Father," Mama began the great prayer. Harriet struggled to say the words with her, "who art in heaven." There were too many words, but they were sweet—honey-sweet.

Harriet let herself float on the sea of prayer words. Now and then she said a few of them with Mama. "Thy will be done . . ." "daily bread . . ." "the kingdom, the power, and the glory . . ." Now and then she napped between words. The prayer was so long!

Daddy's voice woke her. "The Lord is my shepherd . . ." He was saying a Bible psalm, but Harriet drifted away before he finished.

* * * *

Over the next few weeks, Harriet gathered
strength. When she was awake, she heard
about the months she was so sick. "We took
turns spoon-feedin' you," her brother Robert
said. "Mama kept soup simmerin' yonder,"
He gestured toward the smoky fire on the
floor in the middle of the cabin. "Folks kept
it freshened with new meat. Squirrel or possum. Fish. Even rabbit. Nothin' be too good
for our Harriet."

"Mama wiped your body clean near every
day," Henry said. "You looked like a starved
kitten, girl—but a clean one."

"Others brought cloths, too, and helped
Mama with your care," Harriet was told.
"Brodas's other slaves, the Saturday night
folk, church friends, and the minister, too.
Little Mary Ann here"—Brother Ben
pointed to Minty's niece, sitting nearby—
"took to watching over you as you slept."
Mary Ann smiled, showing great gaps in her

teeth. "Even the shopkeeper dropped by to see you alive."

"Did he get away safe?" Harriet asked one afternoon. She didn't even want to say his name. In case he'd been caught near the Bucktown Store. Or later. In case he got killed for running after all. After what she'd done for him—and what had happened to her head. It would be too awful if . . .

Her family members looked at one another. Suddenly the room was full of silent smiles. Harriet said a quiet prayer of thanks. She was alive. And he got free.

"I don't know how to say this," her brother told her another day. "Master Brodas is talking about selling you off. He says none of us is worth a lick for worrying about you." He laughed. "He's probably right."

Harriet began sobbing. "Please, Dear Lord," she prayed aloud, "don't let my master sell me South."

"No, no, Harriet." Her brother patted her shoulder. "Don't upset yourself. It won't happen."

Oh, God, change his mind. Don't let Master sell me. Please, God. The prayer repeated over and over, but silently now, in her head. *Make him act like a true Christian, God.* She prayed as she staggered to the outhouse. She prayed as she sat up, resting in the spring sunshine. She prayed as she eased herself back down on the straw mattress. God, she knew, would answer her prayers. Hadn't He let her live when Mama begged Him?

"There she is. You name what you think she's worth." Master Brodas strode across the dirt yard with a strange white man.

"Her? With her head all stove in like that? I wouldn't take her, nohow," the stranger said. "Not even if you paid me." Then he laughed and shook his head. Mr. Brodas stamped away after him.

Harriet closed her eyes. Every bit of her felt cold, down to the bone. *It is true,* she thought. *Master is selling me. And God . . .* a new thought made her want to howl with emptiness. *God is not even trying to save me.* She thought about being marched off the farm and out of town, naked and chained to strangers. Like Sophie had been. Like Linah. She could hear the chains clank.

No! Anger roared in her head and burned in her gut.

"Kill him, God," she whispered. "Kill Brodas before he sells me." That became her new prayer. It was a terrible thing to ask for, she knew. But it made her feel better to say it. Besides, a prayer was just words. She had probably gotten better all on her own, with Mama's help—not God's. And He hadn't changed Brodas's mind when she'd prayed for that. *Kill him,* she prayed, knowing the very prayer was evil. *Kill him. Kill Brodas.* Her hatred grew every day. Every thought became, *Kill Brodas.*

* * * *

"Did you hear, Hat?" Henry rushed into the cabin. "Massa Brodas is dead!"

"Oh, God!" Harriet shrieked. "No! I didn't mean it!"

"What you talking 'bout?" her brother held her tight. "Stop your crying. Hush, now, Minty baby." He eased Harriet to the ground. "Hush, little sister." He patted her shoulder. Harriet couldn't stop the screams. They came from somewhere deep inside, where she had let the evil hatred grow. The hatred that had called on God to murder a man.

Henry stood up. "Stop it, now. Stop screaming." He ran out the door. "Mama! Mama, come quick! Harriet done lost her senses!"

Harriet couldn't stop crying. *What have I done?* She punished herself endlessly. *Oh, Lord. I killed him. I killed him.* She couldn't do anything but weep before this all-powerful God who had been listening to her prayers, after all. *I killed him with my prayers,* she told herself. *I am guilty. Of killing Brodas. Of doubting God.* She didn't know which was worse.

"There, there, dear." Mama's arms were around her, rocking her. "Hush-a-baby. Things will be fine. It's in God's hands." At that, Harriet cried all the harder. "You try, Ben," she said to her husband.

"We belong to Old Master's son, now." Daddy's deep voice cut through the tears. "Nobody goin' be sold just now."

That wasn't the problem, but Harriet couldn't tell her father that. She could never tell anyone. She had killed Old Master Brodas just as surely as if she'd held a gun to his head. She began crying again.

"Young Master Brodas be too little to own slaves, hisself," Papa went on explaining. "Another man has charge of us for now. Dr. Thompson. He goin' rent us out around here and earn money. So," he finished, "we all stay here, praise God."

Was there no end of tears? *Forgive me, God,* Harriet's soul screamed as she cried herself to sleep.

She awoke from a horrible dream of running, running from horsemen. Harriet shook herself and wandered out into the sunlight of the slave yard. She stretched. Somehow she felt better. Much better. Wide awake and refreshed. Dizzy, of course, and weak, but the sun warmed her skin, and the dust felt soft under her feet. Long strings of geese honked high over head, heading north. A wren scolded from a new nest under the eaves of the cabin. It was all so pretty and alive.

Harriet's stomach grumbled. *Cracklin' bread would be good, and molasses. And some bacon.* He mouth watered. The feeling of longing for food felt strange. *How long has it been,* she wondered. Harriet gasped. *I am being told to eat*. God, the all-powerful, wanted her to eat. Harriet shook her head. Even after what she had done, God wanted her to live. He had forgiven her! *I'll never doubt you again, Lord,* she prayed. *Never.*

"Why, Hat, you put that broom down, girl!"

"I got to help you some, now." Harriet slowly pushed the twig broom over the floor of the slave cabin. "It's time, Mama. I can't stay sickly all my life." She reached out to steady herself against the log wall.

Mama nodded, glancing at Harriet's head. "Keep goin', Minty-baby. Seems the Lord is protecting you." She turned to leave. "I gots work to do. Seems you do, too." Then she was gone.

Harriet took a deep breath and unwrapped the cloth that covered her hair. Slowly she reached her hand up to the center of the pain in her head. Her fingers felt a deep dent by her hairline. Beneath the hair and the slick skin of a scar, she could feel raggedy bumps of bone. The other side of her head was smooth. She tried not to think what she must look like as she retied her head cloth and finished sweeping.

She rested a moment, then carried the wooden slabs and spoons out to the creek. She settled into a patch of sunshine on the bank. *Keep goin'*, she told herself, making her arms move. One by one she scoured the dishes with handfuls of clean, wet sand and a flat stone. Harriet was almost panting with the work. She felt weak, but after the smoky, stale air of the cabin, the honeysuckle scent of summer tasted sweet in her mouth. Dragonflies darted back and forth over the creek, catching mosquitoes. Overhead, gulls screamed as they glided free in the air.

"Mind if I set awhile with you?" Robert asked. Harriet patted the mossy spot next to her. Her brother sat down. "Shore is good to see you up and movin'. Never seed your hands empty before . . . before . . ."

Suddenly the air was full of the sound of singing. From overhead, the gulls cried, but there were others calling, too. Across the field beyond the creek, women in long dresses stretched their arms out toward Harriet. "Come," they called her. "Come." They seemed to want her to cross a line. To come away. To join them. "Harriet!" a deep voice commanded.

"Hat? Hey, Hat!" Robert's voice was louder than the singers', closer than the deep speaker. Suddenly, the singers were gone, and the field empty. Harriet blinked.

The creek was back. The dishes. Her brother. "I saw . . . ," she said, searching for words.

"Minty-baby, you just dozed off, sitting right there." Her brother stood and offered her his hand. "I help you back to the cabin so you can lie down."

"No," she said. "I be fine. I didn't sleep,

Robert. I saw . . ."—she pictured the beautiful women—"I think I saw . . . angels. They had to be angels. And they wanted me to . . ." She stopped. *If those were angels, then the voice had to be . . .* It was just like visions in the Bible. Minty closed her eyes in awe.

"Fine," she heard her brother say. "If you want to rest right there, that be just fine."

"No," she said, struggling to her feet. "Wait."

He helped her gather the plates and spoons, their wood gleaming pale and smooth in the sunshine. He didn't say a word to her as they walked to the cabin. Harriet didn't mind. She needed to think. *What did it mean?* She knew she hadn't been asleep, because she didn't remember waking up. She knew what she'd seen, clear as daylight. Loud as seagulls. And beautiful . . . the memory took her breath.

* * * *

Harriet looked at the mound of ashes

heaped under the cook fire. She wouldn't need pots of soup kept hot anymore. She scraped the ashes away and scooped them into a shovel. Then she carried them out to the ash barrel by the barn. Later they'd be needed to make soap. She leaned against the fence post, weary. Her muscles felt watery, and her head roared with pain. *Jus' keep goin'*, she told herself.

Her little niece skipped from the cabins to join her. Mary Ann was old enough now to be wearing clothes. Her thin shift flapped against bare brown legs. Chickens fluttered out of the way, scolding. Harriet was scolding herself, too. For three months her family had had to care for her, work where they'd been hired, and do the work around the cabin, too. Soap making, cleaning and cooking, garden tending, washing, sewing . . . the list went on and on.

It was time she shouldered her own load, she thought. *No.* The decision came, firm and strong. *I got to do more than my share. I got to make up for all that's been done for me.* She thought of all the folks who'd helped— family, slaves from all over, the church. Somehow she would repay them all.

Harriet sat on the edge of the horse trough and wiped her eyes. Her energy was so low. The headache wouldn't quit. But there was no way she would lie down again. Not now. The sound of hoofbeats made her look up. Horsemen in dark cloaks thundered into the farmyard. Screams filled the air. The raiders reached down from their saddles, grabbing children and babies. Mothers shrieked and sobbed. Babies wailed in terror as the horsemen carried them away. "Where are you taking them?!" Harriet screamed. Dust swirled in the air as one of the riders galloped toward her. His ice-blue eyes met hers for an instant, then he was gone.

The slave yard was empty. Mama's hand was shaking her shoulder. "Wake up!" Mary

Ann patted Harriet's skirt and looked up, her dark eyes full of worry.

"Minty-baby!" Mama's voice called. "You back with us?"

"It's jus' like I told you," Robert said to Harriet's mother. "She don' know she sleepin'."

"I'm not," Harriet said. She swallowed to get the feel of dust out of her mouth. "I am seein' visions." Mama and Robert backed away. "Things I am meant to see, like Moses with the bush all afire."

"Come back and lie down, baby," Mama said. She looked at the ash shovel in her daughter's hand. "Sick as you been, you be doin' too much."

"You believe me, don't you?" Harriet looked from her mother's face to her brother's and back. Their eyes were full of kindness and love, but Harriet could see they didn't believe.

Mary Ann just looked terrified. "Mama!" she cried, and ran toward the cabins.

If more visions came, Harriet realized, it might be better to keep them to herself. *But how can I hide visions,* she argued with herself. *They be miracles, sent straight from God above.* She rubbed her aching head and decided to be very careful who she told about her precious secret. *When will the next one come?* she wondered, and smiled as she picked up the ash bucket.

Her Own Woman

"Just wait till you see what my runty little slave can do!" Mr. Stewart bragged.

Harriet pressed her lips together and kept walking. She hated the man who'd hired her out this year. She hated Dr. Thompson, too. Young Master Brodas's caretaker was working the slaves harder than Old Brodas ever had. Harriet hadn't been home to the cabin in weeks.

"Get over here, Harriet." Mr. Stewart wasn't done. Harriet shuffled toward the group of men on the front porch. She kept her face blank and tried to plan a trick. She knew what was coming. He would ask her to pull a wagon, or lift a barrel, or split a big old cottonwood log with one swing of the ax—anything to show off her strength.

"Yes, Massa?" she mumbled, keeping her eyes down.

"This darky works a full day in my fields and still can cut half a cord of wood before the stars come out."

The men came down the porch steps and towered around her. "Her?" one of them sneered, poking Harriet's arm.

She made herself stand still and look stupid. Inside, she grinned, thinking about the money she was making with all those cords of wood. Dr. Thompson had hired her out to Mr. Stewart for forty dollars a week, the normal fee for a woman's slave labor. Any money she earned after Mr. Stewart's work was done was hers to keep. She never spent a penny. She saved it all to buy herself free from Dr. Thompson.

"Show them, Harriet," Mr. Stewart said. "Haul that bale of tobacco leaves off the wagon."

"Ain't no way a little chil' like her kin do that!" one man snorted.

"Care to place a bet? That 'child' is about twenty, and strong as you," Mr. Stewart said quietly. Harriet did not stay to see how many of them wanted to put their money down. She walked silently to the wagon, then hauled the bale toward the edge by the cords that bound it. The warm, honey-sweet smell of aged tobacco leaves filled her nostrils as she leaned her shoulder down. *It can't weigh much more than I do*, she told herself. *It's just a matter of balance.*

"She'll kill herself," one man called out.

"Harriet. You want to do this for me?" Mr. Stewart called.

Harriet straightened, keeping her eyes down. "Yassuh, Massa, I does," she mumbled, and bent again to the task. She heard the bets being doubled. The load rolled onto her shoulder, and she staggered once before she forced her legs to straighten. It helped to think of the money and how soon she would be free—free of this place and free of men who could order her around, poke her whenever they wanted, or whip her when they felt like it. The rage made her strong.

Once the bale was even, the weight pulled the muscles of her back and thighs, but she forced herself to step straight across the front yard. As she turned the corner, she heard hoots and groans from the bettors.

Harriet was out of their sight, but she kept going. She carried the bale into the barn and dropped it right on a pile of rotting cabbage. The stink of rot mixed with the sweet tobacco scent. Harriet thought it smelled grand. Dusting off her hands, she strode out toward the field.

* * * *

"Why, sister Harriet," the farmer said. He tipped his hat. "Don't you be telling me you want my babies already?"

Harriet laughed. Together they watched the calves grazing in the pasture. Great blackflies buzzed about their heads, but the calves only flicked their ears. "Nothing stops them when they're eating," the farmer said. "Good thing, too. These oxen are goin' be monster big." He looked her up and down. "Why, in a couple'a years they be twice as tall as you."

"They'd better be," Harriet answered. "They going to pull me all the way to freedom." She glanced at the farmer. His skin was just as black as hers, but he'd been free all his life. He owned this land. That barn. The ox. They, at least, would soon be hers.

After she counted out forty dollars of her wood-chopping money, the farmer asked, "You want me to help yoke them?" He put the money in a deep pocket in his overalls

and added quickly, "Not that you need help, Harriet. Everybody hereabouts knows you be strong. And stubborn," he added with a laugh. "Now they'll know you be rich, too."

Harriet let herself grin as they rounded up the calves. They frisked away, then quieted as rope halters snugged down on their heads. The training yoke, carved of birch, was light. When they were full grown, they'd need a huge oaken yoke. As the wood settled on their shoulders, Harriet and the farmer took turns pushing the collar pieces up around the calves' necks. When the pins were all in place, the calves dipped their heads again and went back to feeding.

"Walk by the team's right side," the farmer said, handing her a switch. "They'll be tame as puppy dogs." He backed off and looked at Harriet with her new livestock. "They better be, you bein' so tiny-like." She glared at him. "And strong," he added.

Harriet walked her team for miles down

the dusty roads that evening. Slaves and free blacks came to their fences to admire them.

"Daddy!" she cried when they were finally home.

Ben came out of their garden, wiping his hands on a rag. Mary Ann came running, too. She was as tall as Harriet now. "Ain't they the sweetest little ones!" She rubbed her fingers through the curly hair atop their heads and scratched the fluffy spots behind their ears. "Aunt Hat, I jus' been asked into the doctor's big house. Think of that!"

"I cain't say I like the idea," Harriet said. She watched her niece's face fall. "But that be me," she said quickly. "This child wants to spend my days out in the field—or in the woods with my daddy."

Ben smiled at her. "You know how much timber we can haul over to the mill with a team like this?" he said.

"Daddy. They're just babies now. But they can start training tomorrow evening with small logs."

Harriet loved working with her father. He knew the moods of the woods and its animals. He could follow trails and tracks through the densest swamps or open fields. He knew how to find the best fishing holes, ripest berries, and biggest nests of fresh quail eggs. Every evening for years he had shared his secrets with her.

Their owners thought the two slaves were simply cutting a little wood in the forests south of Charlestown. Without speaking about it, Harriet knew her father was teaching her how to hide. How to survive. How to run away, if she ever decided to go.

The North would welcome her now, if she could just get there—but the risks were great. So many slaves had run off that owners were hiring people to patrol the nights, watching for escaped slaves. These "pattyrollers" got paid a reward for every slave they caught. The penalty for running away was torture.

Runaways were whipped or burned or branded or cut by their owners. Sometimes the slave's family was tortured, too.

The masters did it as a warning to all the other slaves. They wanted to be feared. It made Harriet angry, but it also made her afraid of even trying to escape. In any case, as bad as things were with Master Stewart, there was no reason to run just now. Unless Dr. Thompson decided to sell her, it was safer just to keep working. In a few years there would be money enough to buy her freedom, and she could live anywhere she pleased.

"Care to dance?"

Harriet jerked awake at the invitation. She looked around herself. This wasn't a vision. It was the grove of trees down beside the river. The night was hot. The day had been long. She had just wanted to rest her sore muscles and listen to the Saturday drums.

"Are you the famous Harriet? The pretty little slip of a woman who drives full-sized oxen all by herself?"

Harriet felt a flush creep into her cheeks. She had to think for a minute to remember his name. "John?" She'd seen him now and then at the hoedowns.

"John Tubman, freeman," he said, sticking out his chest. "Now put the day's work behind you, girl. Dance with me a piece, an' then we'll go ridin'." He waved his hand toward the edge of the road, where a horse grazed quietly in the traces of a wagon.

Harriet glanced around the crowd. Most of the girls her age were busy tending their babies. The lucky ones had chosen their husbands. Others had been given husbands by their masters. The whites wanted them to start having babies early. That way they'd get a big crop of young slaves to work their farms—or to sell for cash.

Ole Master Brodas hadn't planned a marriage for her. She'd always thought it was because she brought more money working as a slave. But part of her wondered if it was because of her head—or the visions that kept coming. Would any man ever want a woman like her? And John wasn't just a man. He was a freeman. . . .

"But . . . ," she began to protest. Didn't he know she was a slave?

"Young Brodas won't care a lick," John interrupted, "so long as you keep bringing in the cash he do so desperately need. Now, dance."

Harriet found herself laughing as she took John's hand. "You have some nerve," she said. She liked how her friends hooted and pointed at the two of them. John strutted like a rooster when she was by his side. When they moved apart in the circle dances, he dragged his feet and whimpered. When the dance brought them back together, he put his hands on her waist and picked her right up like she was thistledown.

Those hands are free! Her heart beat fast as a rattler's tail in her chest. *John is free, and*—she couldn't miss all the signs—*he is courting me! Me!* Every time she thought about it, her breath came quicker. The long day was forgotten. Harriet's muscles were strong again, and fresh. Her feet invented wild new dance steps.

Finally they stopped, panting, for a dipperful of cool, sweet water. Little puffs of wind tossed up sparks from the bonfire. "My, my," John said, his gaze following the sparks upward. "Them fireflies sparkle like your eyes when you be dancin'." Light from the bonfire glinted bone-pale along the sycamore trunks and flickered on the undersides of a thousand rustling leaves.

"I've never seen it like this before," Harriet said. It was easy to talk to this freeman. *Free. Man.* It echoed like a heartbeat in her mind. "Look." She pointed toward a break in the leafy covering. "There's a star!"

"Let's get into my chariot and go chase us down some stars." Laughing, they headed for the wagon. Outside of the trees, the wind was stronger. "Might be a storm coming," John said.

Harriet climbed silently up onto the wagon seat. John gave a laugh, untied the horse, and jumped into the wagon beside her.

"You're wet as a drowned rat!" Mama scolded when Harriet finally got home. Rain pounded on the roof of the slave cabin.

"Oh, Mama!" Harriet gushed. "Dancing with John felt like dancing with freedom itself!"

"Minty-baby," Mama Ross clucked over her daughter. "You keep your eyes open, honey. Tricksters come in all shapes. You hear what I say?"

"He is a good man, Mama. Me being strong don't throw him off like it does with some boys. He likes it that I drive oxen." In the glow of light from the cook fire, Harriet could see Mama was shaking her head. "And

Mama, he saw me get a vision. That didn't bother him, neither." Mama was still silent. "He doesn't even care about my head. I think I want to be with him."

Mama put her hand over Harriet's. "Nothing on this here earth can change your mind when you choose a path, baby. You better be asking God 'bout this. He alone knows if this is a good thing to think about."

Over the next few months Harriet prayed, and she spent time thinking—when she wasn't dancing. John Tubman showed up on all the Saturday nights. He came to the church services, too. He helped her drive the team to the sawmill with their load of logs. He said he was proud of her when she got paid good money for her work. It made Harriet's heart soar.

"Dr. Thompson." Harriet stood in the front parlor of the Brodas house. Young Master Brodas slouched in a chair nearby, looking bored. "I be askin' . . ."—Harriet didn't know who to ask, so she spoke to the space between them—"well, can I be marryin' John Tubman?"

Dr. Thompson looked at Master Brodas. The young man shrugged. "I s'pose so."

"Yes," Dr. Thompson said. "You can live with this John Tubman on the weekends if you like."

Yes! On the inside, Harriet was dancing and singing. She couldn't wait to tell John!

"But," Dr. Thompson went on, "you best not forget one thing. Your husband may be free, but you are still a Brodas slave."

Harriet stared at the carpet. *Only until I buy my emancipation,* she thought. *Once I get freedom papers, I be my own woman.* The joy of it kept her going day after day.

"Oh," Young Master Brodas said, finally smiling, "and all your little babies will be mine."

One starry Saturday night, Harriet and John came dressed clean for the hoedown. After the cloths were spread, the food covered, and the children quieted down, John brought out a ring for her. Harriet looked at him in surprise. She knew he earned enough money to buy her a real ring. This one was hammered from a copper penny. It was what a poor slave would give his bride before they jumped over the broom together and became man and wife. A freeman like John should have a proper ring— and a wedding ceremony in a church!

"I could have paid for one," he said, sliding it on her finger, "but I made this special for you." They made their promises and prayed for the Lord's blessing on their marriage. Then Harriet and John held hands and closed their eyes. John's hand felt warm and strong in the cool night air. Behind them, she knew, her brothers would be holding a broom.

"Higher," someone said. "Just lay it on the ground," another voice suggested.

"Ben," she called to her youngest brother, "don't you be movin' it as we jump, now." The warm laughter of family and friends swirled around them. Harriet ached to peek before she jumped. *What if I fall?*

"I never seed you scared of nothin' before," her brother Moses teased.

"Go on," Henry said. "I'll make sure the stick is level."

Harriet squeezed John's hand. She felt him bend down, so she got ready. When he jumped, so did she. Harriet had to lean on John for balance, but they landed on their feet. Their friends whooped and cheered. Mama and Daddy and all their relatives crowded close to hug the bride.

"You be Harriet Tubman, now, Hat," John said. "How do that sound to your ears?"

Harriet knew that the ceremony wasn't legal in the courts of Maryland, but it was the only kind of wedding that the slaves were allowed. To all of them now, she and John were husband and wife forever. Harriet knew it to the core of her bones.

"Dance with me," John said.

Freedom!

"Another eight have gone North, John." Harriet swept the cabin she shared on weekends with her husband. "That makes more than two hundred from this county gone free just this year."

"How you know that, Hat?" John tipped his chair back and lifted his feet so her broom could reach the week's dust. "A pattyroller might have got them. They could all be dead. Starved in the woods. Lost." He picked his teeth. "My shirt needs mending."

Harriet threw her broom into the corner.

"When I'm in the woods, cutting, I hear things, John. I know things." She stamped into the kitchen. "There's plenty of safe places," she called back to him, "and people who would help. A Quaker lady stopped me in the street just yesterday. She gave me directions to a house that helps slaves escape just two days' walk from here. I could go North and be free, too."

"Don't be foolish." John brought his chair down with a thud on the wooden floor. "What you want to go riskin' your life for? You have me."

Harriet felt in her pocket for a slip of paper the woman had given her, and shook her head silently. She wouldn't show John. Five years of marriage, and he still didn't understand. She leaned over a pan full of sizzling fish.

"Mmmmm, smells so good." John had come up behind her. "You feed me just fine, Harriet." He patted her shoulder.

"Nice you had a day for fishin'," she said, thinking about her day: hours planting in a farmer's fields, hours more cutting and hauling wood in the forest, then putting the tired oxen up for the night and walking to her husband's house. *My house,* she tried to tell herself.

"And tomorrow night we put the hoe down, Hat. I get to show off with the prettiest little woman in Dorchester County."

"Don't you try sweet-talkin' me!" Harriet said, but she smiled as she put dinner on their plates.

"Oh, I dearly do love dancin' you round the fire," John went on. "Your eyes flash like the stars themselves."

It was the kind of thing he was always saying when she got angry with him. She couldn't even start to complain before he swept her away with his loving words. *The worst part is,* she thought, *it always works. He is almost like a trickster.* She put the idea right out of her mind. "I need your help, John," Harriet said, scooping greens onto her plate, and grits she'd baked. It seemed a good time to ask a favor. "I put aside five dollars." She ignored his angry cough. "I want you to take it to a lawyer up on High Street and ask him to look into my papers."

"Is that all you think about, Harriet? Getting free?"

Harriet made her voice stay low and calm. "Please, John." She didn't want to walk up past the steps of the county courthouse herself. Slaves were bought and sold there, stripped naked when the owners chose, bargained over, and led off in chains. Slaves like Linah and Sophie. *It could still happen to me.* The thought made her shudder.

"I'll do it," John grumbled. "But I could sure use that money for a passel of other things."

"Hat, you purely will not believe what the lawyer found out for you," John said several weeks later.

"What?" She looked up from sewing a rip in her work dress.

"Your mama is free." Harriet stared at him and slumped in a chair on the porch. He was making no sense. "Rit should be free, by rights. Sixty-five years ago, your mother's first master died. His will gave your mama to somebody named Mary Patterson."

"I know that much," Harriet said. "Miss Patterson be a good mistress, to hear mama tell. But she died young."

"Well, Hat, Miss Patterson left a will that nobody troubled to tell your mama 'bout." Harriet waited. She could hardly breathe. "That will," John reported, "it said your mama only had to serve until she was forty-five—unless Miss Patterson died. Then she would be free."

"Mama never knew that!" Harriet's mind raced. Not only had Miss Patterson died, but Mama was much older than forty-five. Mama was free! Harriet gasped. That meant her

children were, too. They had labored under the lash their whole lives. Her brothers should all be free—and their little children, too. Linah and Sophie, in chains somewhere down South—they should be free. For once, Harriet's deep, husky voice failed. "I'm free," she whispered. "I've always been free. Me." It ended in a thin squeak.

"Take it easy, Hat," John said. "The lawyer told me there ain't no way Brodas is goin' to agree to any of this."

"But—"

"Ain't goin' happen, Hat."

Harriet knew that was true. There was no way to fight this. No slave could afford to take an owner to court. No court would agree to emancipate slaves, making them free forever—not here, not now, when slaves were running away so often that the farms were suffering for lack of labor. A bitter taste rose in her mouth.

"All Miss Susan's lashings." Harriet's voice

was quiet, flat, and dead. "Gettin' my head broke in. Doin' them stupid tricks for Master Stewart." Her voice was rising. "All the overseer's whips. None of it had to happen, John."

Harriet rubbed her scarred neck. She wanted to scream with rage. She wanted to throw herself to the floor and sob in sorrow. She wanted to take justice on every cruel master she'd ever had. Her fists clenched at the thought of whipping each one of them for every time they'd whipped her. Her hands clenched around the whip handles. Her arms trembled with strength. With anger. If she could get a gun, she thought . . . she pictured shooting Miss Susan first. The screams. The blood.

Harriet staggered backward. What was she thinking? *Oh, God,* she prayed. *Please keep me calm.*

"Hat?" John asked. "You having a vision?"

"No." Harriet took a shuddering breath

and fell to her knees. "I'm praying," she mumbled to her husband. *Help me, God,* she begged. *Don't let the hate take over again.* Her breathing slowed.

She knew why John had asked about visions. She'd had many of them lately. The horsemen had been coming for her by day. They awoke her at night, too. "They're coming, they're coming!" she would scream into the darkness while John tried to comfort her. The beautiful white women had appeared, calling her over a line. Other visions had come, too, but that wasn't where her mind was now.

Now she was trying to stay calm. Knowing she was, by law, free. Knowing she was, in fact, still a slave. Knowing there was only one way out.

North.

"John, I've decided," she finally answered. "With or without you, I'm goin' to run."

❖ ❖ ❖ ❖

"Young Massa Brodas is dead."

It was March of 1849. Harriet stared at the slave who had brought the news to the field. As the word spread around her, wailing filled the field of young tobacco sprouts. Harriet felt like crying, too. Young Brodas had been a good master, letting her keep the extra money she had made. He—or his father, or even Dr. Thompson—had never been cruel to her. They were good men.

Fear made her feel like crying, too. What would happen now? Would Master Brodas's wife keep her slaves? Or would she sell them?

Within days Harriet heard the answer. One of the house slaves had heard the plans. Mistress Eliza Ann needed cash. There would be a sale. Not Harriet's mama and Daddy—nobody would pay much for them, anyway. But the younger children . . . the strong ones . . .

It was time.

"I be runnin' after sunset," she told her brothers across a row of tobacco. "You comin'?"

They looked at each other. "What about your husband?" Henry asked.

Harriet gazed off across the field. "John will not come," she said. Her voice felt tight. They had only used words on each other, but that last fight had hurt like a whipping. *Only it is worse,* she thought. *Words like that cut deep. Specially when they come from some-body you love.* She swallowed back tears.

"Does Mama know you're goin'?" Ben asked. "She goin' cry and carry on something terrible."

"No. That would give us away," Harriet said. "Daddy gave me wood skills; Mama taught me to plan—and to pray. They know I can make it."

"I got to think," Ben said. "Leaving them here . . . and all the others . . ." He looked slowly around the wide, flat field full of slaves. "What is it like up North? What do we do when we get there?" His voice dropped. "*If* we get there." When the overseer cracked his whip, Ben bent quickly to his work.

"You be sold if you stay," Harriet said. "I'll meet you by the river. Bring what food you can."

"You have to let Mama know," Ben said.

A slave began singing on the far end of the field. Others joined in the song. "I'll leave word," Harriet promised. "She'll understand by and by."

Harriet had decided how to say good-bye long before she left. That evening she put on extra layers of clothes. She tucked all the money she had in her pocket along with the Quaker woman's paper. Sunset was coming, pink and gold. When it was time, Harriet took a deep breath and strode out toward the river.

"When that old chariot comes," she sang the old hymn as she walked past the slave cabins, "I'm going to leave you, / I'm bound for the promised land." She let her rich voice fill the soft pink sky. "Friends, I'm going to leave you."

One or two of the slaves stepped out into the twilight to watch her. "Nice evening," Mary Ann called. Her sweetheart stood beside her.

Harriet didn't stop walking—or singing. "I'm sorry, friends, to leave you, / Farewell! oh, farewell!" She had picked the hymn carefully. It was about dying, perhaps, but it said just what she wanted to say tonight. "But I'll meet you in the morning, / Farewell! oh, Farewell!"

The evening star glowed brightly in the west as Harriet walked past her own folk's cabin. "I'll meet you in the morning," she sang. "When you reach the promised land; / On the other side of the Jordan, / For I'm bound for the promised land."

Suddenly her brothers slipped out the door and grabbed her arms. "I can't risk this," Henry whispered.

"And I'm not ready," Ben told her. "I need a day to think more."

"We can't let you go this way." They led her into the cabin. Harriet tried to pull away, but it was too late. Mama had seen.

"Look what we found," Henry said. "It's Hat." Harriet forced a smile onto her face for her mother. "Mama, she'd like a bite to eat," Henry said. "You got extra possum stew?"

No! Harriet wanted to scream. *What have they done? My plans are ruined!* She glared at them both.

"Harriet, what's wrong, honey-child?" Mama asked. "You be trembling like a hare in a fox den." *She knows me too well,* Harriet thought. She made her breathing slow. She couldn't run now. Mama would raise a ruckus for sure. Harriet looked at her mother. The woman's hair was going gray, and her back was stooped. *She's lookin' old*. Harriet sniffed the good, rich smell of Mama's stew. *I do want to stay a bit, now that I'm here*, Harriet thought. She settled down to the floor beside her father.

Mama had given her a clue, Harriet realized. *Think like trickster Hare*, she told herself. Her brothers might have trapped her for tonight, but she would have another chance to escape—so long as she wasn't sold away tomorrow.

Harriet watched her brothers. She wouldn't be telling them her plans again. Anger flashed, until she prayed it away. They would just have to stay slaves until they ran on their own. Ben and Henry sat on the dirt floor, laughing and joking with Mama and Daddy. They didn't seem to notice a new plan forming in the old cabin.

❖ ❖ ❖ ❖

Harriet pretended everything was normal through the long Friday night.

"Milking time," Mama said the next morning.

Harriet's heart bounded like a rabbit. *There's my chance,* she thought. "Mama," she lied. "I'll go and do the milking for you!" *Forgive me,* she sent a quick prayer skyward, put on her sunbonnet, and began her escape.

By the big house, Mary Ann skipped out to join her. "Where're you going?" she asked.

Harriet thought quickly. Mary Ann was more than just kin. This niece had become a real friend. She could take the message now and wait until later to tell Mama good-bye for her. But before she could explain anything, the Master arrived on his horse.

"Oooh!" Mary Ann squealed, "Here comes the doctor! He best not see me talkin' like this!" She ran back to the house.

Harriet swallowed hard. She wasn't going to change her plans again. But she wanted to say good-bye. Her legs trembled with excitement. *This is it.* Staring right at the doctor, she started to sing. "I'm bound for the promised land." Her voice got stronger as she went, swinging the bucket in time with the hymn. "Farewell! oh, farewell! / I'll meet you in the morning / When you reach the promised land; / On the other side of the Jordan."

She walked straight toward the cows in the field. Instead of stopping to milk the near one, she dodged around it, finishing the song, "I'm bound for the promised land." Keeping the cow's body between herself and the master, Harriet dropped the bucket and ducked into the cornfield. Keeping her head lower than the cornstalks, she sprinted down a corn row. Harriet climbed through the fence at the far end of the field. As she passed into the cool woods beyond the fence, she hurried to hide in the shadows.

Alone

Harriet glanced up toward the sun. How could she get away in broad daylight? She said a quick prayer, tucked her skirt up into her waistband so she wouldn't trip, and ran down a narrow path. After years cutting wood in the forest with her daddy, she knew what trails to take. It would be hours before her mistress knew she was missing, and she hoped to be deep in the Greenbriar swamp by then. Because of all the snakes and the mosquitoes, the knee-deep mud and the stories of swamp ghosts, not many folks would chase her there.

Where the ground was soggy wet, Harriet picked her way carefully. Where it was dry and firm, she flew, leaping over logs and ditches. Every time the path turned toward a road or open field, she took another turn, back into the woods. She sprinted past the store where she'd been hurt so badly, and the Methodist church. The white lady had stopped her on the road near here with directions.

"Get thee to the end of Choptank River," the lady had told Harriet, using the word "thee" instead of "you," as Quakers always did. "Thee will find Camden town and a white house with green shutters, and help will be there for thee."

A new sound broke into her thoughts. Harriet strained to hear. Off in the distance was a faint rattling and squeaking, and a steady clop-plopping. *A wagon,* Harriet thought, *and it is coming closer!* She ducked behind a holly bush and held her breath. The plop, plop, plop of horse's hooves on the dirt road never slowed. Harriet listened until the sound had passed. Until it vanished in the distance. Carefully she stood up, ready to duck out of sight again. She thought about what might happen if she was caught. It would be much worse than a whipping. So many slaves had escaped lately that when the masters caught one, they were especially cruel. They cut off the runaway's ears, branded their face with a hot iron, or even hung them, as a warning to their other slaves. When she was certain the wagon had passed, Harriet sprinted on.

The flat land grew soggier and the grass taller as she neared the swamp. The trees hung thick with vines. Jaggedy thorns on the greenbriers tore at Harriet's legs. She picked her way carefully into the swamp, but didn't stop. *Keep goin',* she told herself when her feet sank into thick, gooey mud. When the mosquitoes bit, when the hornets stung, when poison ivy itched and burned, she repeated,

100

Keep goin'. What's ahead gots to be better than what's gone before. Great white birds squawked and flew free into the sky as she pushed on. A muskrat stared at her, then dove into the swamp water.

At last the sky began to fade. With darkness came safety, and Harriet pushed on out of the swamp and past fields of tomatoes, corn, and beans. She stopped at the Choptank River and looked back. No one was following her. All she could hear over the beating of her own heart was the gabbing of hundreds of geese settling in for the night. The river was coming up high with the tide and smelled of good, rich mud.

From deep in one pocket she pulled an ashcake and nibbled one edge. The hot coals of the cook fire had toasted a sweet taste right into the cornmeal. It was cold now, but it was food. She made it last, then chewed at a strip of fat. The grease in the bacon answered the hunger she had tried not to listen to during the day.

Harriet licked her fingers, pulled her skirts up over her knees, and waded into the river mud. High tide would cover her footsteps soon. No scent would be left for dogs to follow. She shuddered, imagining their frantic barking—and their sharp teeth.

Moonlight glinted on the water and mud. Harriet followed the river north through the night, listening for danger. She did not feel tired. She was heading for freedom, at last! As the night passed, the moon set. Harriet left the low, flat country of Maryland. Now the ground was drier, and the great Choptank River narrowed down to a brook. Delaware land was different: slow rises followed low hills. The creeks cut in deeper. Harriet had to be careful not to slide in and twist an ankle.

The stars sparkled over everything. Daddy had shown Harriet the North Star when she was just a baby. She'd grown up looking at the stars of the "drinking gourd" every night, and the shimmering wash of the Milky Way across the heavens. The sky was as much her home as her cabin had ever been, she thought. But she would never have to leave the sky. *Thank you, Lord,* she breathed, staring upward. The morning star glowed for hours before dawn, then the sky brightened.

Where were the roads in this strange place? Where were the trails where she could be seen by a passing farmer—or a slave-catcher? It was safer to rest in the daylight. Harriet settled in behind a huge log. Her skirts were wet and mud-caked; her feet, sore; her legs, scratched. As she sat watching a family of chipmunks racing over stumps in the woods the sunlight flickered. Great swirls of color fell around the log. Harriet crouched down. "Come," she heard the angels, though she could not see them. "Come. We are ready." Then they were gone, and the colors with them. Harriet stretched her arms skyward and praised God.

As soon as it was dark and safe to travel she

headed north along the creek. Finally the Choptank was just a trickle, and then it was gone. *Keep goin'*, she told herself. She knew where north was and walked that way while the moon rose. By its pale blue light she could just make out a dirt road. *That has to be the way to Camden*, she thought, and said a quick prayer for safety. She crept along through the deep grasses beside the road. First she saw one house. Then another. A dog barked. Harriet froze until he was silent again, then moved even more carefully. A cluster of homes sat nestled beyond a rise.

Which one was white with green shutters? Harriet strained her eyes, but in the night, the colors were invisible. At dawn's first light she looked carefully to make sure which house was safe. She crept to the door, took a deep breath, and knocked softly.

"Who goes there?"

Harriet could barely hear the voice. It was a woman's voice. A white woman's. Harriet knew the words to answer. She had repeated them in her mind over and over so she would never forget. But now the time had come, and she couldn't make herself say the words. Not to a white woman.

The dog began to bark again. "Hush thee, Spot," a man's shout made Harriet jump. Spot kept barking. Lantern light glowed from a window next door.

"Who goes there?" the woman behind the door asked again, softly. "Be bold, friend. Hurry."

The woman had called her "Friend!" Harriet could breathe again. And she could give the secret answer. "A friend of a friend," she said, quietly.

The door jerked open. A tall woman reached out, pulled her inside, and shut the door behind her. "Welcome," she whispered. Harriet blinked in the bright candlelight. She pulled out the paper from the Quaker lady.

"Well, Harriet," the woman said, looking at

the paper, "I am Mrs. Hunn. Thee can rest here, safe, for a few days. Thee must be hungry."

Harriet, empty beyond hunger, ate and ate then climbed into a soft bed with clean sheets and a feather pillow. *A bed such as Miss Susan sleeps in,* Harriet thought. She looked around for the bedside whip. There was none. There was just softness and the scent of flowers, and soon, deep sleep.

For the next three days Harriet stayed in the house, talking with Mr. and Mrs. Hunn. "This is but one stop on the vast Underground Railroad," Mr. Hunn explained. "All over this country there are people who feel slavery is wrong. They break the law and hide slaves from their owners and the patrollers."

"Do you all know one another?" Harriet asked.

"No, no," Mrs. Hunn said. "We only know

of the next stop on the path to freedom. Someday we might be caught at this. We would have to tell everything we know to the court. It is better that we know little."

"Thee will find that most of the houses like this one are run by free blacks," Mr. Hunn said. Harriet thought about the whispers she had heard on Saturday nights. It began to make sense. Why, she knew of two Underground Railroad stops near her own home! Now she knew not to say anything about them to the Hunns or to anyone else.

After three days Mrs. Hunn gave Harriet clean clothes and a packet of molasses cookies for the next part of her journey. Mr. Hunn drove her part of the way after hiding her under the potatoes in his wagon. He told her to walk north for two days until she reached Wilmington, then to wait in a graveyard outside the town.

❖ ❖ ❖ ❖

Harriet snuck into the graveyard at dawn. A strange figure was walking back and forth, muttering. Harriet felt the hairs on her neck stir. *A ghost haunting its grave?* She hid behind the biggest gravestone and held her breath as he passed.

"I have a ticket for the railroad," he was saying. "I have a ticket . . ."

This was no ghost! "Sir?" Harriet stood up. The man stopped and greeted her by name. He led her to a wagon and handed her men's clothes to wear into town. "I can't wear the clothes of a man," she said. *What is wrong with him?* she thought. No woman ever wore pants, just like no man ever wore skirts.

"They are looking for you, Harriet. If you wear these clothes and pull this workman's hat down over your scar, they might not know who you are." Harriet hurried into the new clothes. The man drove her over the bridge into Wilmington. It wasn't hard for Harriet to remember to keep her face down. She had never seen so many carriages and buggies and wagons in her life! And the people! Black and white, rich and poor, babies and dogs—it made her dizzy to look at them all.

"This is Mr. Garrett's store, Harriet," he told her as she got out. "He will take good care of you."

Harriet the "workman" jumped out of the wagon and walked into the shoe store. "Would thee care for tea?" a well-dressed shopkeeper said, peering through spectacles at Harriet's paper. She was astonished by the invitation. Take tea with a white man? And then *he* poured the tea for *her!* Harriet was speechless.

Two days later, dressed as a "fine lady," she climbed into a buggy. Now she wore a new dress. Her face was covered by a long, elegant veil that hung from a fancy hat.

Mr. Garrett had given her the very first pair of shoes she'd ever worn. They were real leather, and black as a moonless night. He'd given her a buttonhook, too, and shown her how to use it to pull all the tiny shoe buttons through the holes he'd made in the leather. The shoes pinched her feet and they squeaked, but they were hers to keep. Harriet wanted to smile whenever she looked down and saw them peeking back at her from under her long skirt.

"Head through those woods, Harriet," Mr. Garrett said as he led her out later.

She handed him back the hat. "God bless you and keep you, sir," she said. *How many travelers have hidden under that veil?* she wondered. She knew not to ask.

"The free state of Pennsylvania is less than a full day's walk from here," he told her, and showed her the mark to look for on the border roads. "But be very careful. This area is the last chance for patrollers to catch runaways and earn their rewards. They are looking for you, Harriet."

✳ ✳ ✳

The morning dawn filled the sky with peach and yellow. Harriet yawned, but pushed on. The border had to be nearby. She crouched and ran along the edge of a field, keeping in the shadows. Her feet had been sore all night inside the new shoes. Now that it was growing light, she could see how fine the shoes were. Somehow it made her feet feel better. Meadowlarks sang, but the blue jays hadn't sounded any alarm. She whispered a prayer of thanks. *Just a little farther,* she promised herself. *Then I'll find a hiding place for the day.* A road bordered the edge of the field.

She glanced both ways down the road. No one was in sight. Harriet crossed quickly and ducked down behind a bush. There was a stiff paper nailed to a fence post nearby. Harriet listened for the sound of hooves or feet. All was silent, but for the birdcalls. She stood and strode to the front of the sign and looked. Writing covered most of the paper. Harriet paid no attention to that. Instead she stared at a picture of a black man and woman in chains. *The pattyrollers are here!* She glanced up and down the road, behind her and in front. *Where are they now? Where can I hide?*

She dove behind the bush she'd used before. Her hem caught and ripped, but she just nestled farther into the bramble. Her knee hit a stone. She rubbed the bruise through her skirt and glared at the stone. It was a marker nestled in a patch of poison oak. She stared. Shadows filled a carving in the rock. It was the Pennsylvania mark!

Harriet took a deep breath. This was the line! She had finally crossed over. *I'm free,* she thought. It didn't seem possible, but Harriet had reached her goal. She stood up, right out in the sunshine. *I'm free!* She stared at her hands. They still looked like slave's hands, dark and rough with years of labor. *But they are my own hands now,* she thought. *I can use them to do what I want, when I want. I'm free! I'm free!* It pounded like a heartbeat in her mind.

The sun came up gold through the trees and sparkled on dewdrops everywhere. The glossy leaves of the young corn plants shimmered with the light. Harriet raised her hands in praise to God. She was in a free state, and the sky and the plants and even the dust of the road glowed gold around her. It felt like heaven. *I'm free!*

She looked back toward the south. *All those years,* she thought. *Twenty-nine years a slave.* Harriet wanted to shout, to clap and dance, or to sing joyful hymns, but there was no one to hear.

"I'm free!" She tried saying it aloud. It just sounded lonely on the empty road.

What now, Lord? Harriet wondered. She began walking north in the sunshine. All those years she had dreamed about this moment, but it felt as empty as the road. *I'm like a stranger in a strange land,* she thought, remembering Moses in the Bible.

But being free like this was worse than just lonely. Harriet kept walking as a fear grew inside. *Who will tell me what to do next?* she thought. If only she could talk it over with John. They'd had a terrible fight when she left, but she missed him now. He was smart and strong and always knew what to do. How he would hug her! Harriet shook her head. *He didn't want to come,* she told herself, and tried not to love him.

She thought of her mama and daddy, waking up this very morning, still slaves. Would her brothers be whipped today? Worse, would they be sold? Nothing like that could happen to her now. She was free. But Mary Ann wasn't. And her family . . . Anger burned inside her like a hot coal. *It isn't fair!* All of the slaves she'd ever known were still laboring dawn to dark for masters while she stood in the sunlight, free. *And alone.*

The answer rushed through her. *That* was what she would do: free the others. If she could make her own way to freedom, she could lead others along this trail. She felt the dreadful empty place inside her filling with this new goal. "Thank you, God," she breathed, and fell to her knees, full of strength. "I'm going to hold steady to You," she prayed. "You will see me through."

"May I introduce myself?" The gentleman in the paper-cluttered room spoke right to her. "I am William Still. Welcome to the Pennsylvania Anti-Slavery Society office." Mr. Still was dressed in a fancy black suit. His collar and cuffs were frayed, but were bright white and starched stiff. Harriet looked at the floor. She shouldn't be in this office, her face scarred, and her clothes stained with river water and sweat.

"And what is thy name?" This Mr. Still talked just as fast as everyone else she'd heard in the Philadelphia streets, but his voice was kind.

"Harriet, sir."

"Did thee leave a family behind?" Mr. Still asked.

"My husband." It hurt Harriet to say the words. "John Tubman."

"Then thee will need a job and a place to stay," Mr. Still said. "I can give thee money for food, too."

"Thank you, sir, thank you!" Harriet gasped. "You are too good."

"Thou must not thank me," Mr. Still said. "The money and the help comes from our many friends in the North who believe slavery is wrong, Mrs. Tubman."

Harriet blinked. A white man had called her "Mrs."! She stood taller. It took a moment for her to realize he was asking her questions. Yes, she told him, she could cook, cut wood, tend fields, or dig ditches. She said she would rather not work as a housemaid or care for babies.

"Can thee read?" he asked. Harriet simply

shook her head at the foolish question. Didn't he know slaves could be killed for learning to read—or teaching it to others? "Can thee write thy name?" Mr. Still asked, as if she might say yes. "No matter," he said. "I have a job for a dishwasher in the hotel right down the street. Here is some money for food until payday this Friday."

Harriet wondered if she was dreaming. This was no vision. The coins lay hard and heavy in her hand.

"If thee will step over here," Mr. Still prompted. They walked across a thin carpet to a huge black steamer trunk. "I'm sure we can find thee fresh clothes." He opened the lid to show her layer after layer of skirts and shirts, petticoats, pantaloons, head cloths, and men's clothes, too. Harriet gasped as he handed her an armful. "From the churches," he said, "and abolitionists across the country."

"Praise God," Harriet mumbled a prayer. "Praise the Lord." It was all she could do as

Mr. Still repeated the directions to her job. And her room. And a store where she could buy food.

"God be with thee, sister," Mr. Still finally said.

"Oh, He is," Harriet answered. "He most surely is."

Prayer helped Harriet through the next months as she learned how to be free in a Northern city. Everything was different from home. With the help of her new church and friends from the hotel kitchen, she discovered how to buy soap instead of making it, and how to wash her clothes without a river nearby. She learned how to buy food instead of raising and butchering animals herself, and how to live without a cook fire handy on the floor near her bed. She stopped being afraid of the gaslights in her room and the streetlights outside her window all night.

Some things didn't change. Visions came

to her, even in the city: angels, dark-cloaked riders, brilliant lights, and strange, holy voices. "We threw cold water on you," a friendly voice said one morning by the hotel sink, "but you wouldn't wake up nohow."

Harriet looked around. The cook, Ethel, was talking to her. The rest of the kitchen staff stood in a ring, staring. Harriet shivered in her wet shirt. "Do you be sick, honey?" Ethel asked.

"No," Harriet chose her answer carefully. "I jus' get spells. Been like this most all my life."

"Who-eee! God must love you, child." The cook's voice was full of wonder. "You run all the way from Maryland, even with a handicap like them sleepin' spells?"

"Pure grit," the washwoman said. "You is made of willpower."

"I jus' keeps going," Harriet mumbled. She wished they wouldn't make such a fuss. The spells were gifts from God, not a handicap.

And of course He loves me. He loves every-one. The talking swirled around her.

"That's it," someone else was saying. "You looked like you was a'sleepin', sudden-like." Their stories tumbled one over the other. "I even tried a'pinchin' ya." "'Bang!' I shouted it right in your ear, and you didn't turn a hair."

"Funny thing is," Ethel said, "when I said your name, quiet-like, you came right back to us." Then: "Land's sake—look! The noodles are boiling over!" Suddenly everyone was busy again. Harriet could get back to her dishes.

"I quit," she told her first boss.

He had talked to her one day like she was a slave. Like she was stupid. So she quit.

And for once, her boss couldn't whip her. He wasn't her master at all. He couldn't chain her to the sink or threaten to sell her South if she didn't work. He couldn't do anything to make her stay. This was the North, and she was free.

It felt like heaven. Down the street was another hotel, and another one beyond that. Philadelphia was full of jobs. Harriet could work anywhere she chose. She could wear what she wanted and live where she chose. She could even talk to anyone, out loud, in plain sight, in the middle of the day.

Why did I wait so long to come runnin'? she often wondered. Then she would remember the fear. She knew the everyday terror and shame that stayed with a slave, sunup to sundown. The slavery just went on into nights of horror.

And her family was still suffering. She longed to let her family see freedom. To taste the power. Harriet carried the ache with her everywhere. *Dear Lord, keep them safe.* As she peeled potatoes, or washed tablecloths, or stirred stews, she thought about her family. *Where are they right now?* She could only guess. Mama and Daddy were probably safe in their cabin. Henry, Ben, Robert, and the rest of her brothers would be working the fields. *And Mary Ann?* She was getting to be so pretty. Had the doctor made her marry someone? The idea made Harriet's temper rise. *That shouldn't happen to anyone!* But it would—and soon. Her little niece would be making slave babies for her master any day now. *Poor Mary Ann!* The more Harriet thought about it, the angrier she got. *Someone has to save her!*

Me.

There was no other answer.

But she couldn't do it alone.

Dear God, she prayed. *I have enough money saved. Thank you for that. I am well. I am strong. I am Yours. I am going South for Mary Ann. My life is in Your hands.*

Amen.

Moses

"Go back to Maryland? Thee can't be serious!" William Still stared at her.

"How can I stay here?" Harriet said, right back at him. *I sound different,* she thought, *like John.* Loneliness washed over her at the thought of her husband. She made herself go on. "My family is still under the lash." Harriet tried to listen to her own raspy voice instead of her sad memories. *I don't sound like a slave anymore,* she thought. She stood taller and went on. "I've got to go get them."

124

"But, Harriet, thee were lucky to get out alive once."

"The Lord showed me what I have to do. I put my trust in Him."

"We have no money to help thee just now. . . ."

"I saved every penny this year, Mr. Still. I have enough." Mr. Still was shaking his head. "That be my plan," she told him. "Work till I have enough. Sneak back and fetch someone free. Then start right in savin' for the next trip."

"Harriet, I will do whatever I can to help." Mr. Still's voice was low and serious. "Thou art the bravest soul I have ever met."

"Harriet!" Mary Ann whispered. "When I heard you singing, I could not believe it be you. We all thought you be dead." She hugged her aunt tight.

"I'm not dead," Harriet said. "I'm free! I know how to get to free Yankeeland. I be back to lead you there." She looked around the clearing behind the outhouse. "Meet me here Saturday, sunset. The doctor won't look for you till Monday. Even if he hears 'bout your escape, he can't get posters made on Sunday. The pattyrollers know nothin' 'bout us till Monday. And this weather"—she gestured around at the snow falling through the December night—"will make it hard for folks to get out after us."

"But, Harriet"—Mary Ann sighed—"I cain't leave everybody I love." She took a deep breath. "Let my folks come, too, and show the way. Then we run."

Harriet wanted to shout with joy. God's plan was going to work! "Wear extra clothes," she said, "and wrap your feet thick in rags. Sneak what food you can."

"Saturday is two days yet, Harriet," Mary Ann said. "Where you be hidin' till then?"

"Can't tell."

"You do sound changed," Mary Ann said.

"I be my own master now." Harriet glanced toward the big house. There was no sign of the doctor, but she knew to move on. "I got to go visit my own home."

"To John's house?" Mary Ann put her hand on Harriet's arm. "You don't want to do that."

"What you talkin' 'bout? He be my husband. He will come when he knows it be easy to get work in Philadelphia."

"You be coming back for your mama?" Mary Ann asked.

"By an' by," Harriet said. "Why you ask?"

"'Cause this ain't no time to see John. Go see your daddy, instead."

Harriet thought about it. Maybe it *was* too soon to go back to John. He had been so angry when she'd left. He had said things she never hoped to hear again. She could see him the next time she came home.

Harriet found her brothers. They snuck her into the cabin when her mama was out.

"She give you away, sure as dogs got fleas," Henry said.

Papa Ben had a cloth tied over his face when Harriet walked into her old home. "You hurt?" She said, running to hug him.

"No, Minty," he said. "But this way, if Master say, 'Ben, did you see Harriet?' I don' have to lie. 'Cause I ain't seed you at all." He gave her an extra squeeze. "But you sure 'nuff feel good to me."

"I can't do this, Harriet," Mary Ann whispered. An owl hooted in the trees beyond the big house. Mary Ann jumped as if it were by her elbow. "I'm not brave like you."

Harriet shook her head. *She's only been a house slave*, she reminded herself. *She knows parlors and kitchens, not swamps and starry nights.* "Nothing out here will hurt you," she said again, "except pattyrollers."

"Oh, no!" Mary Ann's voice trembled in the night. Her brothers muttered.

128

"Hush," Harriet scolded. "Nobody be looking for us. Not yet. Now, move!" Pushing and pleading, scolding and shushing, Harriet finally got Mary Ann and the others to the banks of the Choptank. "Stay low. Keep walking in the marsh grass," she said.

"But I'm tired." "The wind cuts through my coat." "My feet are wet." There was no end to their complaints.

"Do you want to be free?" Harriet challenged.

"Yes, but can't we stop now and rest a bit?"

"Children," Harriet snapped, "if you are tired, keep goin'. If you are scared, keep goin'. If you are hungry, keep goin'. If you want to taste freedom, keep goin'."

They slogged silently for hours through the marshes beside the river. Finally Harriet let them stop to eat some of the salt pork, corn, and cold baked yams they'd brought. She left her cold bacon in her skirt pocket to chew on later. "Now," she said as she started walking again, "follow me." Harriet tried not to hear the tired whimpers.

Dear God, this is hard, she prayed, then: *Please give them the strength to get to Pennsylvania.* Harriet's feet just kept marching through the cold afternoon. Would it always be this hard to get slaves out? Why weren't they hurrying to be free? Harriet remembered her first escape. She'd been scared; afraid of what she would face if she escaped, and afraid of what she would face here if she didn't. With that much fear and anger inside her, she couldn't stop.

Mary Ann walked slower and slower in the endless, raw winter wind. "When we take supper," Harriet told her quietly, "I'll tell you all 'bout Wilmington city. How it be to wear shoes every day. How to pick work to do. How sweet to quit when the boss say, 'Boo!'" Harriet paused. "I even be telling you how to dress like a man or pretend you be a white lady."

"Harriet! Now you be making up lies!"

Mary Ann sounded horrified, but the anger made her steps stronger. "Nothin' would make me do such things!"

Thank you, God. Harriet smiled inside. Now she knew one way to keep a body moving.

"I'm through," one of Mary Ann's brothers said a few hours later. He sat down on a log, unwrapped the rags around one foot, and rubbed it. "It's too cold and too far." He glared at Harriet.

"Can't let you turn back now," she told him. "They find you, you be givin' us all away." The man didn't move. "Get up." She tried to make him angry enough to move. "Get goin'. You actin' like a baby."

"You can't make me."

Harriet thought quickly. She had to scare him into moving, somehow. But he was big. What would make him move? She needed a plan as clever as Anansi's. The spider could always trick the biggest animals. Harriet stuck her hand deep into the pocket of her skirt. *Forgive me, Lord,* she prayed. Then she lied. "I have a gun. I shoot you if I have to. Now, get going." She twitched the packet of bacon toward him, and prayed, *Lord, make him believe me.*

The man's eyes got big as he stared at the bulge in her pocket. "Go forward and live," she said, her voice low with warning, "or turn back and die." He got to his feet. "Don' make me use this," she threatened. Mary Ann's brother finally started moving north. *Thank you, Lord,* Harriet said silently. She made up her mind to get a real gun to carry on the next trip North, just in case.

She needed the gun to keep people moving on her next trip south that spring. Her brother Henry came, too, and a couple of other slaves. "I heard that owl call of yours, Harriet, and you singing, too. "Swing low, sweet chariot," Henry sang a few words of the gospel hymn, then stopped. "Sister, do you know what people been calling you?"

Harriet shook her head. They should be walking, not talking in the soft rain.

"Moses. They be callin' you Moses." Harriet smiled inside, thinking of it. "And they say that song be written just plain about what you be doin'. You be the chariot comin' for to carry me home."

"Hush your voice," she scolded. "You be givin' us to the pattyrollers with all your singin'." She shut her eyes and shook her head. She shouldn't be feeling this proud. It was the Lord, after all, who made all things possible. Not her. She was just a slave girl.

"Harriet!" Henry's voice called her back. She looked around, blinking. Where was she? Her brother helped her off the ground beside the road.

I fell here, she thought, *out in the open? What if a pattyroller had seen us?* "Hurry," she said, leading the way off the muddy road and toward the river. "Follow me!" The urge was strong. The vision had shown her great danger. She waded into the water.

"Where are you going?" frightened voices called. "I can't swim!" "Harriet, no!"

But Harriet walked steadily into the river, her long skirts drifting with the current. The water was knee-deep, then waist-deep, then shoulder-high, and still she kept walking. The mud below her feet grew firmer and the water shallower, and then she was on the far bank. "Hurry," she called. Wet and frightened, they followed her past a bend in the river to crouch, silent, in the tall marsh grasses. "Silence!" she hissed.

Through the reeds they watched a group of white men ride down the road across the river. "They have to be here!" one of them yelled.

"Keep looking," another man called, shielding his eyes from the rain. "I want the reward money."

"Especially for that Moses. He'll bring a pretty penny!"

"He must be quite a man," the first one said.

"Naw. He's just a nigger like all the rest."

No one in the reeds moved. Each of the pattyrollers carried a gun. Slaves knew that they were loaded with birdshot, not bullets. Shot never killed clean. Instead, dozens of little pellets tore into the flesh. Each metal pellet could fester and kill, unless they were first dug out. That took time—and, live or die, it was torture. Either way, the pattyrollers got paid, in cash.

Finally Harriet said, "We be safe."

The group cautiously got to their feet. "How you know they be coming, Harriet? Or that the river be shallow enough to cross?"

Harriet silently stood and wrung what water she could from her skirts. *How can I tell them the Lord showed me exactly what was comin'—and jus' what to do 'bout it in a vision?* she thought. *I can hardly believe it myself*. Saying nothing at all, "Moses" moved the men North to freedom.

Months later, in 1850, the Fugitive Slave Law passed. It said that runaway slaves could be chased anywhere in the United States. It didn't matter how far slaves had run. It didn't matter how many years they had lived free, either. If a pattyroller or a lawman found them, they could be taken from their families and children and hauled back to their masters in a slave state. It took a while for the news to spread.

"Did you hear about the riots down in Christiana?" The streets of Philadelphia buzzed with the news. "The master came ridin' up to Pennsylvania to get his slaves back?" "With a U.S. marshall?" "What happened?" "How many of our kind attacked?" "And abolition-men, too? Praise God!" "The master himself got killed, dead?" "Hurrah!"

Escaped slaves and free blacks gathered on the street corners, sharing news. "Oh, Lordy," one woman said, "think on it. This mean they be comin' after us now in free states, too."

A street sweeper leaned on his broom. "Whites kill slaves every day," he said. "Nothin' happens to them. I say we got a right to kill us some whites." The crowd pulled away from him.

"Do this new law mean we all got to go back to runnin'?"

"Yassuh. All the way to Canada."

"I'm heading home for more slaves," Harriet told William Still. "How do I be takin' them North from here?"

"Haven't thee done enough, Harriet?" he asked, gazing at her face. "No, I didn't think so. Well, thee must take thy passengers on to New York City from here. Then thee must follow the grand Hudson River north to

Albany city. From there it is overland and west to Niagara River. Thee can cross over to Canada and safety at a town called Niagara Falls. It is a far longer trip, and hard—and with new danger at every step."

"There's two things I have a right to: death or liberty," Harriet told him. "One or the other, I mean to have."

"What if you're caught?"

"No one will take me back alive. I will fight for my liberty. When the time is come for me to go, the Lord will let them kill me."

William Still shook his head in wonder, then told Harriet that more money had come into the antislavery offices. People in the North were more upset about slavery since the most recent Fugitive Slave Law had been passed. They had seen good black citizens of the North—carpenters, ministers, sailors, and churchwomen—marched back to the South in chains.

"There will be train tickets and a safe house

waiting on thy return," he told her. "But know this: A Patty Cannon in Maryland has turned on us. She says she is part of the Underground Railroad and has spread the word far and wide. But when slaves knock on her door, she has them arrested. Then she gets the rewards. This seems the devil's work."

Harriet headed back to Maryland, warning everyone about Patty Cannon. "Be sure," she said. "Be very sure you know the way if you start North. There may be more snakes like her, hiding along the trail."

Harriet meant to free her brothers and sisters this time, and she wanted to bring John back with her. As she neared town she saw Master Stewart heading down the street. Suddenly she wished she'd waited until full dark to come to Charlestown. If he looked at her in this twilight, he would recognize her in a heartbeat!

Thinking quickly, Harriet grabbed a couple of chickens from a yard and kept walking.

She hunched over like a little old lady. Mr. Stewart didn't seem to notice her until the last minute. His footsteps paused, and Harriet let both the chickens go. She faked a high squeal of anger, and the chickens clucked and fluttered wildly about. Harriet bent down farther, chasing after them this way and that. Her squeaky voice called, "Here, chick, chick. Here, chick!" but her prayer was *Thank you, Lord!*

"Out of my way, you stupid, old darky," Mr. Stewart cursed, and hurried past her. Harriet smiled inside. Stupid? Old? The smile kept her going all the way to the house she'd shared with John Tubman.

Harriet crept along a row of trees. Voices floated through the open window in the quiet evening air. Harriet froze, listening. There was John's dear voice. She breathed quicker, just hearing it. But two or three strange men were there, and a handful of women, too. They were having dinner,

laughing and talking loudly. *Our friends*, Harriet thought, recognizing some of the people inside. *And strangers.* Fear tingled through her. *Hide!* She slid down a tree trunk to wait for them all to leave—all but her John.

Two by two, the guests walked off into the night. Harriet ducked her head so her eyes couldn't reflect the glint of starlight in the shadows where she knelt. Finally it was quiet. Harriet rose, straightened her skirt, and retied her kerchief. Taking a deep breath, she walked softly to the front door. She licked her lips and knocked.

John threw the door open. "What?" he stared at Harriet as if he didn't know who she was.

"I'm home, John." She smiled.

John moved to block the door. "Ah, Harriet . . . ," he said. He sounded strange.

Harriet pushed past him into the room— her room. A strange woman stood before her. "Harriet . . . ," John began. "Harriet," he tried again. "This, ah"—he put an arm around the stranger. "This is my new wife. A real one. Married in the church, with papers. . . ."

Harriet could not remember how she got out of the room, or into the woods, or to the shore of the Choptank. She didn't know how her skirts—or her cheeks—got so wet. The angels came to her that night, and other visions, too, but it wasn't until dawn had streaked the sky with pink that she could trust herself to pray. *Don't harm him, Lord,* she said carefully. *But be with me. I am so alone.* There were no more tears to cry, so she made plans, instead.

This time she headed North with nine slaves. The next trip she took six. One was a baby who cried in her basket until Harriet gave her a strong medicine. The child slept all the way to Pennsylvania, on up to New York State, and all the way to Niagara Falls, Canada, and to freedom.

Harriet worked as a free woman in Canada during the summer. She worked in hiding in Cape May, New Jersey, or in Philadelphia, Pennsylvania, during the winter. Every bit of extra money she earned went toward her next trip. Spring and fall, she would sneak back into Maryland, singing her presence through hymns. "Steal away," she sang in the woods outside of towns. "Steal away to Jesus." Slaves knew to gather at the next new moon or at the first of the month.

"You mean to tell me a white man led an attack on slave owners?" Harriet stood in William Stills's office.

"Thee knows that a Quaker never fights, Harriet. Never."

Harriet nodded.

"I cannot say that John Brown has done a good thing—and I will not have you thinking of him as a hero."

But he is! The more Harriet heard about

this John Brown, the more she loved him. Four of his sons took part in the raid at Pottawatamie Creek in Kansas. *He risked his own life, and his sons did, too, for my people!* There was no end to the wonder of it. *He killed five men who owned slaves, before he took off into hiding. Praise the Lord,* Harriet prayed. *Protect this man John Brown.*

Harriet continued to labor, bringing souls to freedom.

Famous people asked to meet the brave woman. Frederick Douglass, an ex-slave who had learned to read and write, had wandered the North speaking against slavery. He thanked her, himself, for the hundreds of people she'd freed. A lawyer from Illinois, Abraham Lincoln, was talking against slavery, too. He argued that all slaves, everywhere in the country, should be free. The idea thrilled abolitionists and blacks everywhere. It horrified slave owners. Harriet had another hero.

When she was in the North, abolitionists asked her to speak in churches and rich people's homes to tell about her experiences. They collected money after she spoke and sent it to fight slavery. Some of the money she raised went back to William Still, and some remained in her own hands for her next trip South.

Harriet passed more and more posters as she snuck through the slave states. She never learned to read, so the posters she passed offering forty thousand dollars for the capture of "Moses" meant nothing to her. Her own hometown, Charlestown, had lost so many slaves that they passed a law making even free blacks back into slaves again. And still, Harriet kept conducting her people North.

She spoke at a women's rights convention in New York with Elizabeth Cady Stanton and Susan B. Anthony. These women were trying to change the laws that said only men could vote in the United States. Harriet told

146

the audience what happened to women slaves, and why they should get to vote, too. A senator from New York, William Seward, had run a stop on the Underground Railroad in his home in Auburn, New York. After Harriet had stopped there for years, he offered to buy her a home for herself and her family in Auburn.

One summer John Brown visited Harriet in Canada. When she tried to tell him how she admired what he had done in Kansas, he shushed her. He called her "General Harriet" and said she was "one of the bravest and best persons on the continent." He told he was planning to start the war that had to be fought to end slavery in the United States forever. He wanted her help. Harriet was thrilled. He needed funds, and she could raise them. He also needed a leader to organize the slaves to attack at Harpers Ferry, Virginia. If slaves stole all the guns from the army base there, John Brown told her, they could fight to free more slaves. As more and more ran away to join them, their army would grow until freedom couldn't be stopped. John Brown's sons would be there fighting. So would he. Would she help?

"Yes!" she said. "When the time comes, I'll do it!" This war was coming, whether the Quakers wanted it or not. Everyone knew that, but it took a brave man to come out fighting. A brave man like John Brown.

At last, only Harriet's parents were left on the farm in Maryland. They were old now, and so weak, they could hardly walk to town. There was no way they could hike through the wintry nights all the way to Canada. So Harriet stole a horse and made a wagon from boards and a couple of wheels to get them on their way. For the first time, she had to travel right down the roads where pattyrollers could easily find them. But all along the way, Harriet had friends who helped, and in a few weeks, Ben and Rit and Harriet arrived safely in Saint Catharines, Canada.

Harriet was ill when, two years later, the message came from John Brown. She couldn't travel to help him fight. She was still sick when he attacked the military post at Harpers Ferry. She waited in bed to hear the rest of the news. John Brown and his followers were trapped in a firehouse. Robert E. Lee had come to fight. The army won the battle. Two of John Brown's sons were killed in the fight.

"Poor, poor John!" Harriet wailed in sorrow for her friend. Less than two months later, John Brown was hanged for treason. Many people wept. But many others cheered.

Tension between slave states and free states had never been so high. It seemed war had to come—and soon.

In 1860 brave young Abraham Lincoln was elected president. Women could not vote.

Neither could free blacks, or slaves. White men across the country had chosen him. But the Southern states refused to be a part of any country he ruled. One by one, they left to form their own, slave-owning country. They called this new nation the Confederate States of America.

In 1861 they attacked Fort Sumter, and the War Between the States began.

Fighting for Freedom

"Mama"—Harriet looked at her mother, who was wrapped in layers of blankets and hunched by the stove.—"Would you like to move South?"

Mama shivered as another wind shook the little house. It was dim in the living room. Snow piled halfway up the windows, and frost covered the rest. "To Maryland?" she asked hopefully.

"No, Rit," Ben said, rocking in his chair. "You be free here in Canada. Now the war finally got started, you be free in Yankee states, too. No more pattyrollers seeking out runaways. But go back to Maryland, you be a slave all over again."

Harriet watched a shudder pass through her mother. "No, sir," Mama said, "I ain't never going back to that. Never."

"It's not as cold in Auburn, Mama."

"Is there fighting in New York?"

"No," Harriet said. "You'd be warmer there, and safe." Both of her parents nodded, so Harriet went on, explaining her new plan. "I have so many friends there who would help you. Every home in Auburn has welcomed runaway slaves—even when it was against the law."

Mama smiled at the thought.

"With you both safe there, I could go back down South and join the fight." Harriet said it quickly, then held her breath. *What would they say?*

Mama covered her face with her hands.

After a long moment Ben laughed aloud.

"Harriet"—he rocked fiercely in his chair—"You've never been one to sit quiet and let others have the fun."

"Or get the glory," Mama added.

Harriet smiled inside. She was going to war! She could be a spy and sneak about dressed as a man again, or carry her gun and lead troops, or help slaves escape—maybe even help her own sisters escape from a farm down South. That made her smile where everyone could see.

"Oh, help me!" Harriet rushed to a bedside just as the black man began throwing up. She grabbed a tin bowl and tried to catch as much as she could. "Nurse! Nurse!" Cries came from the other side of the tent.

Harriet wiped her forehead and straightened her head cloth. The heat in Fort Monroe was terrible. She looked out of the canvas flap down the row of tents baking in the South Carolina sunshine. The Union army brought all the newly freed slaves here, where they could be safe. She'd been cooking for the camp for months, feeding whole families of ex-slaves.

Before that, she'd nursed wounded Union soldiers in Florida. The army didn't pay her, so she went home to a cabin nearby each night to make gingerbread and pies. She sold them to the soldiers and made enough money to live. With the change of seasons, the white soldiers had started to become ill and die. The tents filled with men whose bodies were covered with blisters. "How can you nurse soldiers with smallpox?" she was asked. "Aren't you afraid you'll catch it yourself—and die?"

"I can't die but once," Harriet explained. She knew God would let her keep going as long as He wanted her to. Then He would call her home. She had nothing to fear, so Harriet feared nothing.

✵ ✵ ✵ ✵

She looked at all the men in this new infirmary. It was all fine for the Union army to bring thousands of runaway slave families to a safe place, but there wasn't anything for them to do on the Carolina coast. Like in any crowded tent city, some of them got sick—and the sickness spread quickly through the water and the air. Harriet had said she could help. It was bad in the women's infirmary, where children were suffering, but the men's tent was the worst. These men could all have been out, healthy and fighting for their own freedom, if they weren't trapped in these tents because of their black skin. She knew all the reasons the army gave. Southern soldiers would kill them for sure as escaped slaves if they were caught. None of these men had ever held a gun. There were no black officers to lead them, either. Still, it didn't seem right.

"Thank you, sister." The nearest soldier patted her weakly and lay back on his cot.

When the post commander walked through, Harriet touched his arm. "I do know how to make a tea to stop the worst of this sickness," she said. "The wild plants I need grow in the forests back behind the dunes."

"What's your name, nurse?" the officer asked.

"Harriet Tubman, sir."

"It's Moses!" The man on the nearest cot spread the word.

"Moses is here!" the men told one another.

"Who she be?" a man demanded, his English ringing with Caribbean Island tones.

"You don't know?" the answer came down the row. "Moses took near three hundred slaves to freedom, single-handed, she did."

"She don' look like much."

"Moses?" The white commander looked at her sharply. "I've heard about you." He seemed to think for a moment. "I can trust you on this. Go. Get your herbs. My men will get you whatever else you need." Then he saluted her.

"We need to know how many troops the enemy has hidden in their camps beyond the mountain, Harriet."

"You asking me to be a scout, General Hunter?" Harriet's heart raced with excitement, but she kept her face blank as she sang inside, *Bless the Lord!* She imagined sneaking through the forests again, wading rivers, tricking slave masters, and dodging pattyrollers.

"If you think it is too dangerous . . ."

"I been a cook for the Union troops, sir. I sewed their shirts. I did their laundry. I even cured their sick. I been waiting for this."

"If they catch you," he reminded her, "you're dead."

"I lived all my born days—forty years, now—among enemies," Harriet said. "Hiding, running, stealing, planning, fooling them all. I'm not scared. When the time is come for me to go, the Lord will let them take me."

For weeks she scouted for the Union army, bringing back news of secret Confederate camps. She raced ahead of the troops to see whether roads were dry or under water. She found the safest paths across rivers and roamed wide to find farms with food for the troops. Harriet carried a government-issue gun and wore big, loose trousers in the woods most of the time now. Normal long skirts caught on brambles and twigs, and they got heavy with dew or creek water. Besides, it wasn't safe for a woman to travel alone near battlefields—not that she let anyone see her.

Now and then she stopped, suddenly, as visions came to her. Some were glorious; others, so terrifying that she could barely breathe for the fear of God. *Thank you, Lord,* she'd pray, astonished again that He chose to show her these miracles. Then she would go on straight into danger knowing He was with her.

In 1863 President Lincoln declared that all slaves in the United States were free. Slave owners in the Confederate States of America had their own president. They felt that Lincoln's "Emancipation Proclamation" meant nothing in their country. Their own president, Jefferson Davis, led them in the fight to keep their property. They loved their new nation and hated Lincoln for trying to force them back into the old United States. Battles raged across the land as white men fought for their countries.

"Do you think you could find out whether the troops are planning to move soon?" General Hunter asked Harriet.

"Well, I cain't jes' walk right in and ask."

"Of course not . . ." the commander said, then stopped. "Harriet, I never do know when you are teasing me."

Harriet didn't let him see her smile. "I'll be

back in three days," she told him.

It was raining on Saturday night. Harriet knew that some of the Southern soldiers made their slaves come with them to their camps. Her people would be gathering, even in this weather. Saturday hoedowns were the first chance all week that the blacks had to talk to one another freely—even in war. They would be too scared to tell a white Yankee soldier anything, but they would know of "Moses." It seemed everybody did.

Her mind raced. They'd tell her what they knew of the plans. She could even lead some of them back to safety at the Union camp! She smiled in the rain and darkness, thinking of how surprised her commander would be when she arrived back with a dozen escaped slaves. *Contraband, sir,* she would say. She shook her head to clear the water from her eyes. *Pay attention,* she scolded herself. The sound of the storm covered her progress. It also drummed out the sound of singing that could lead her to the slaves.

A sudden clap of thunder was followed by, "Who goes there!" Two shapes loomed in the darkness. Harriet froze. She heard the gurgle of liquid in a bottle. The smell of corn liquor told her all she needed to know.

She shuffled over closer. "I's jus comin' to fine muh massah, suh," Harriet mumbled. "I misses him sumptin turrible."

"The darkies are over to nigger camp tonight," the guard said, and belched. "Get on over there. You better be finding your master." He paused for another swig from the bottle. "First daylight we break camp to move to the front."

"Thank yuh, suh, God bless yuh, suh," Harriet said, ducking her head.

"I wish my boy would find me here," the other guard said. "I tire of buttoning my own jacket." He leaned toward Harriet, breathing liquor fumes. "You want to be my nigger, instead?" He laughed.

"No, suh!" Harriet didn't have to pretend the horror in her voice. "Muh massa needs me!"

"An' those Yankees say the slaves want to be free!" While they laughed together, Harriet hurried away into the night. She had to report this to the commander at once!

Harriet ran several more missions for the Union army. One day she heard great news: the rules were changed. Blacks could fight now!

All the men Harriet had nursed in the camps. All the black men waiting on the sidelines. All the "contraband" slaves freed from Southern masters. All of them could join in the battle to end slavery. Over the course of the war, about two hundred thousand black men joined in the fighting—all of them for the Union.

"Will you sail on a gunboat, firing at Rebels and clearing torpedoes and such in South Carolina?" General Hunter asked. "You ran so many successful spy missions for us, we'd like to reward you. We can give you several men to help contact the locals."

"I'll do it if you get Colonel Montgomery to command," Harriet said. "He was a friend of John Brown's. I trust him."

Within weeks Harriet and 150 black men sailed up the Combahee River under Colonel Montgomery. Huge plantations lined the banks. Harriet stood on the bow of the gunboat, staring at the empty cotton fields. Two other gunboats chugged along behind.

There have to be hundreds of slaves to work this much land, she thought. *Where are they?* She glanced at the colonel standing by her side. He looked tall and very white. *I look like his slave, not a captain in his regiment.* She glanced back at the boat. Metal plates covered the wooden boat, protecting it from bullets, rocket shells, and cannonballs. Sunlight glinted on gun barrels bristling outward in every direction.

164

One young slave sprinted out of the field. Colonel Montgomery raised his hand to wave him on. In the gunboat control room, a sailor pulled a lever, and the shrill steam whistle pierced the air. The slave boy put his hands over his ears, turned, and ran back toward the plantation big house. He ducked behind a wagon and would not come out.

"No wonder they're all hiding, sir," she said. "I would, too." She took a step ahead of him and called out, "This here is Lincoln's boat!"

First one slave, then another, came streaking across the field. "Lincoln's boat!" The word spread like sunshine. "Lincoln." The name itself had come to mean freedom. This was Lincoln's war—and these were Lincoln's people. A mother with twins hanging around her neck dashed toward the boat. Three children scurried behind her. An old woman came running with a pot of steaming rice balanced on her head. "Save me!" she cried.

"Keep goin' if you want to taste freedom!"

Harriet's deep voice carried over the water.

"Stop!" a planter yelled from the top of the field. "Back to your cabins!" He cracked his whip at his escaping slaves. The only answer he got was the crack of a gun from the boat. When he fell to the ground, crowds of slaves followed in a rush to the river's edge. Some came empty-handed. Others carried blankets, chickens, pigs, and tiny babies.

Soldiers launched smaller boats to bring them all in to safety—and freedom. "Don't leave me!" "Take me!" slaves yelled. "Please, Please!" Someone started shoving, and a man fell into the river. "Save him!" a woman screamed. Babies cried, chickens squawked, piglets squealed, and men pushed toward freedom. Other slaves clung to the small boats and wouldn't let them leave. It was turning into a riot!

"Sing to them, Harriet," Colonel Montgomery ordered.

"Yes, *sir!*" She saluted. "Of the whole creation, east and west," she began singing, "our Yankee nation is the best."

A tall, young soldier stepped up beside her and sang along. Harriet glanced up at him and smiled. It was Nelson, a handsome runaway slave who had just joined the army. "Come along, come alone, don't be alarm'd, Uncle Sam will give you each a farm!"

"Thank you, Private Davis," she gasped, between verses. Together they belted out hymns and spirituals and fighting songs. His voice—clear, high, and strong—fit just right against her deep, raspy tones. They sang on and on, swaying together in time to their own music. Soon the crowds began to sing, too. Everybody joined in the choruses. The pushing stopped, and slowly everyone was rescued. For weeks the gunboat sailed up and down the rivers, shelling Rebel troops and rescuing eight hundred slaves.

"Come home." Harriet got a message from

her parents. "We need you."

"Here is a pass," her commanding officer said, handing her an official-looking piece of paper. "It says you are an army nurse and have the right to travel on a troop train all the way home. Godspeed, Harriet. And thank you."

Harriet rushed to the train station. Black smoke was already pouring from the stacks of the troop train. Tiny cinders rained on the platform. *Wait for me!* she pleaded, standing in line. The whistle blew as she reached the ticket window.

"I'm sorry, miss," the man behind the counter said. "You are too late."

Harriet had stood unafraid in battles while bullets whizzed over her head, but was scared now. *What if Mama is dying?* she thought. *Mama and Daddy are all alone up there.* Why had she left them? *They have no money for medicine, and no one to help them.* What had she done? *Please God, let them be safe.*

"I *have* to get home!" she pleaded.

"There, there, miss," the ticket clerk said, looking at her pass. "The next troop transport leaves in just a few hours. Can't you wait?" He looked at her face, then added gently, "You could catch the next train. I'll sell you a ticket for half price."

Harriet just nodded. If she spoke, she knew her tears would break loose. He pushed a ticket through the grill to her. Harriet snatched it and dashed onto the next train. *Mama!* The call echoed in her mind as she sat on a grit-covered bench. She shivered, thinking of all she had been through in the war. It was worth it all—if only her parents were well! The train's engine began snorting, and the whistle blew.

"All aboard that's going aboard!" the conductor called. Harriet felt her shoulders relax. She was headed into the North, where she was safe and free.

"You, there! Girl!" a rough voice startled her. "Where's your ticket?"

She looked up into a conductor's angry face. She handed him her ticket and the pass. He only glanced at them. "Nobody rides half-price on this train!" he said.

"I have an army pass," she tried to explain.

"Throw the nigger off." Another conductor ran to help.

She felt the men grab her arms and heave her to her feet. She was dragged down the aisle and into the next car. Harriet was hurled, headfirst, onto a pile of mail sacks. "The baggage car is good enough for you," one of the conductors shouted, and slammed the door closed.

Harriet's arm was twisted up behind her. Was it broken? *Dear God,* she prayed. *help me.* It wasn't fair! Lincoln had said this was over. She'd fought so hard and so long to be free. Slowly she straightened her arm. It didn't seem to be broken, but the pain was far worse than the ache in her head. Harriet propped herself up against a mail sack and tried to breathe evenly. *The Lord is my shepherd . . . ,* She recited Bible verses as the train chugged north.

And finally Harriet let herself cry.

Old Rit had been very sick, but she was sitting up now. "I'll never leave you again, Mama." Harriet had to be careful of her arm as she hugged her mother. Over the next few weeks Harriet's arm healed.

She was home with her parents to hear the glorious news: On April 9, 1865, after the vast, terrible Battle of Appomattox, the Confederate States of America surrendered. Lincoln had triumphed! The United States was one country again—and all the slaves were free. Yankees and blacks celebrated wildly.

A week later all celebration stopped. People walked about with tears running down their faces, unable to speak.

President Lincoln had been shot dead.

Safe Home

"I have pies for sale." Harriet stood at the servant's entrance to the Seward mansion. "Pies, and fresh, hot gingerbread." The spicy cake wasn't quite hot anymore. She'd carried it a mile through the winter wind, going door to door.

"Come in, Aunt Harriet," the cook said. "Warm yourself by the fire here." She took the war hero's heavy basket and sniffed the sweet scents within. "Apple pie?" she asked.

"From the best dried apples off our trees." Harriet shook snow off her coat and long skirts. "Better than fresh!"

"We'll take one." Cook handed her a few coins and said, "Sit a bit now before you head back." She took a pie out of the basket and set it on the wooden counter.

Harriet sighed as she settled herself into the rocking chair where she always sat at the Sewards'. "Can't stay," she said. "Got to keep goin', you know. One pie more to sell, and a houseful of wanderers to feed back at home."

Mrs. Seward rushed into the kitchen with a swirl of silk skirts. "We'll need an extra pie tonight," she gushed. "The Hopkins are coming, with their darling little Sarah."

"How is Sarah?" Harriet asked.

"Still mourning her sweetheart," Mrs. Seward said. "She is far too young to have lost a love." The three women stared silently into the fire.

Almost every family in America had lost a brother or a son, a husband, father, or sweetheart in the War Between the States. During the four years, over six hundred thousand soldiers died. The wounded and battle-scarred men who did come home would never be the same again. It seemed everyone was in pain.

In December 1865 the Constitution was amended to make every slave a free citizen of the United States. That was a mixed blessing —four million slaves lost the only lives they'd known. Most had no idea how to get a job, buy food, or find housing for themselves. How could they all make it on their own? As for the slave owners, they had lost all of what they thought of as their human "livestock" and, with it, all their wealth. How could they run their homes and farms without slave labor?

The new president, Andrew Johnson, did not agree with Lincoln's plans to go easy on the Confederacy after the war. Lincoln knew it would be best if everyone worked together to reconstruct the roads and bridges, railroads, cities, and farms that had been destroyed.

That way, blacks and whites might see how much they both loved the South. But President Johnson passed harsh new laws for "Reconstruction" that suddenly took money and land away from whites. Northern crooks looking for easy riches wandered about. Millions of blacks, free but without skills or jobs, struggled to survive any way they could. Hatred and violence followed. While many ex-slaves stayed near the countryside and neighbors they knew, hundreds of thousands fled North, hoping for jobs and safety.

Harriet welcomed any of these travelers in her home in Auburn. She fed them and gave them a few nights of shelter.

"Miss Sarah always asks about you." Harriet jumped at Mrs. Seward's voice. How long had she been staring into the fire? She shook herself and got to her feet.

"I don't know why she takes time to hear my silly old stories," Harriet said. She pulled her shawl back around the narrow shoulders of her coat and picked up her basket again. It was empty now, and light—and her pocket bulged with coins. She smiled inside. "You tell Miss Sarah I'll be stopping by her house tomorrow. I'll bring her some of the sweet apple butter she loves."

Harriet's steps were light and quick. Home was downhill from the huge houses of her rich customers in Auburn. They often bought her baked goods, even though they had their own kitchen staffs. The Sewards had ten servants, but they always welcomed their "Aunt" Harriet. She always left with a few extra coins in her apron pocket. In the summer and fall she could sell apples and vegetables from the gardens around her house. Wintertime was harder. Sometimes in early spring she had to ask for money to keep her safe home open.

She thought about the schools for freed blacks where she sometimes sent money. And the church to support. There was so much to do. *Keep going,* she reminded herself. *The Lord will provide.*

Her new church helped her, too. Now she worshipped in the African Methodist Episcopal (A.M.E.)–Zion church. A.M.E.–Zion churches never made blacks sit in the back. Blacks ran the churches. The worshippers didn't just drink the wine and eat the bread—they served it, too. The ministers were black. It made Harriet feel at home to sit among other black people who had been through the war.

She was also glad that these members gave the ex-slaves jobs or ideas where they could find jobs.

"Mama?" Harriet called. She stamped her feet before she stepped into her house.

"Harriet, we have a visitor," Mama said.

A young man sat huddled and coughing by the fireplace. He turned in his chair. "That you, Moses?"

Harriet had to think. She'd seen this face

before, but it hadn't been this thin.

He began to sing, "Of the whole creation, east or west, the Yankee nation"—He broke off in a fit of coughing.

". . . is the best." Harriet finished the line and started the chorus: "Come along! Come along." Now she remembered. The gunboat. The handsome young private who sang alongside her on the Combahee River. "Why, Nelson, is that you?" she asked. "Nelson Davis?"

He smiled.

"Hot tea, Mama," she issued the order. "Stir the last of our honey for his throat."

"It's been done, Hat," Papa said, coming out of the kitchen with a steaming cup.

"Got no family left down home. Got no home, either. Got to thinking about our Moses." Nelson took a sip of the hot brew. "I came here to help you," he said, and fell to coughing again.

"First things first," Harriet told him. "We get you well again."

Nelson slowly gained his strength back. He helped in the garden, chopped firewood, and did house chores that Ben was too old to handle. Now and then Harriet gave speeches about her experiences in the war. That brought in some money—but not enough. Even with Nelson's help, they fell behind in the mortgage payments on their house. Harriet had to go begging again.

"I have just had the grandest idea!" Sarah Hopkins said, clapping her hands together.

Harriet looked at the floor. She had come to Sarah's needing income, not ideas.

"Aunt Harriet, you do tell the most astounding stories!"

"They're not stories, Miss Hopkins. They're true."

Sarah laughed. "They're not just true, they're wonderful!" The excitement in her voice nearly made Harriet smile, too. "And I think people would pay to hear them."

Harriet shook her head. "The gardens are coming up to harvest, soon. I can't leave to go gallivanting all around the country giving talks for pennies."

"But your words can."

Harriet stared at Sarah. What could the girl mean?

"If we publish a book of your adventures, every American would pay to read about their hero." Sarah paused to take a breath, then asked, "What's wrong? Isn't that a darling idea?"

"You know I cain't write."

Harriet's head jerked at Sarah's sudden laughter. *It's not funny,* she wanted to say. That was why she sent money for teachers, clothing, and books to two "schools of freedom" in the South—so other ex-slaves wouldn't grow up ignorant.

"I know," Sarah said. "You can't read, either. But I *can,* Aunty. And I'll raise money to pay to have the book made. The money it makes will go to help you keep the house going. Tell me I can write your stories!"

"They're not just stories, Miss Sarah. They're true," Harriet said, but she was smiling inside.

Sarah Hopkins's book, *Scenes in the Life of Harriet Tubman* was published in 1869. It included a list of famous people who donated money to have Harriet's memoirs printed. It also included letters from her old friends from the war. With the twelve hundred dollars it brought her in the first few years, she was able to pay off the loan on the redbrick house Mr. Seward had sold her. She could fix up the house, too, and she had another celebration.

In 1869 Harriet and Nelson Davis were married. This time it was a legal, church wedding, with flowers, a fancy gown, and dozens of guests. The Sewards came—so did Sarah Hopkins and her family, the neighbors, and all her church friends, too.

"Isn't he a bit young for her?" one guest asked. "She has to be about fifty. I can't imagine he is a day over twenty-five."

"Mind your own business, you old busybody," another guest snapped. "Just look at Harriet. Have you ever seen her look so happy?"

Over the next few years Harriet and Nelson nursed old Rit and Ben as they grew ever older. Whenever it seemed a chore, Harriet remembered the months and months her parents had nursed her through the horrible sickness in her head. Nursing took energy, and time, and, sometimes, money for special food and medicine.

"Nelson, where do the other old slaves go?" Harriet said, looking up from the pile of beans she was shelling on the front porch. "The ones that got no money and no kin to keep them?"

Her husband coughed, then said, "Harriet,

it sounds like you're fixin' to fight another battle." He sat down to help her.

"Would it trouble you if I did?"

"Hat," he said, "I wouldn't love you so if you weren't a fighter."

"Well, to tell the truth, then, there's two problems I want to take on."

Nelson laughed until he coughed, then coughed until tears ran from his eyes. "I just knew it," he finally said. "What are you planning now?"

"Seems we should open our home to the old ones and nurse them. Give them a place to stay safe until they go to meet their Maker." She emptied her apron full of bean pods into a bucket. "Of course we'll need more land than we have now. And more buildings. An orchard. A dairy barn. Perhaps even a brick yard." Her voice picked up speed. "The clay here would be baked into top-grade bricks. Of course, we'd need a furnace to fire them, and . . ." She stopped. Nelson was looking at her with a smile on his face. "Oh, don't worry," she said. "God will provide."

"I could see that coming." Nelson stood and stretched his back, then fought back a cough. He picked up the bucket of bean pods. "And you know I will help you as long as I can."

A chill raced down Harriet's back. Nelson didn't often speak about how sick he was. *Keep him safe, Lord,* she sent out a silent wish.

"Hat," he prompted, "what was the other great problem you and I and the Lord are going to solve?"

Harriet had to smile. "You voted against President Johnson."

Nelson nodded.

"So did Mr. Seward. And every other man I know." Nelson was shaking his head, but she went on, anyway. "The war has made you a citizen of the United States now, free and equal to other men. Nelson, I fought, too. But

184

I can't vote—just because I am a woman."

Nelson was taking the bean pods out to toss them to the pig.

"Well, it's not fair," she said to his back.

Harriet could not do much about her "old folks home" yet, but she could fight for women's rights. She spoke to cheering crowds, and was once introduced by Susan B. Anthony as "Our Conductor."

"That's right," Harriet said in her strong, deep voice, "I was a conductor for eight years. I never ran my train off the track, and I never lost a single passenger." As wild applause filled the room, she nodded and smiled her secret inside smile.

Everyone there knew about her role in the Underground Railroad. They knew how much she had given her country—and how little it had given her in return. No army pension. No awards. Not even the right to vote. She knew that her story made them angry—angry enough to fight even harder for women's right to vote.

In 1875 a farm near her home came up for auction. With the money she and Nelson had saved, Harriet bought the property. Congressman Seward helped again. The property still had a loan on it, but it was twenty-five acres of good land, a fine white house, and a barn—perfect for the Harriet Tubman Home for Indigent Aged Negroes. "My one last work," she called it.

Harriet's parents grew old and died in her loving care in the home. Her dear husband, Nelson, died there, too, of tuberculosis, in 1888. They had been married nineteen years.

What would Harriet do without him? *Keep going,* she would tell herself. As always, she put her trust in God, and he gave her twenty-five more years of life.

Now she was world famous. Queen Victoria sent her a magnificent white shawl. She only wore it for photographs. She left it at home when she toiled up the road toward the Sewards' house with a basket of fresh vegetables or warm pies to sell. Sarah Hopkins published another book of Harriet's stories. It seemed everyone now knew the secrets of the Underground Railroad and its brave conductor Harriet Tubman.

But that did not help Harriet pay the bills. Rather than lose her precious home and put all its patients out on the streets, Harriet gave the property to the African Methodist Episcopal–Zion church to run. She was in a wheelchair when, in the late 1890s, the United States granted her an army pension at last. Thirty years after her service as scout and spy, they finally began to pay her twenty dollars a month.

In 1913 Harriet was ninety-three years old. She was dying, but her will was as strong as ever. She called for her minister and told him what to say. She told her friends what hymns to sing, too. As much as she could, she sang along with them to "Swing Low, Sweet Chariot," and "Steal Away to Jesus." Her last words were, "Give my love to all the churches." On October 10, she joined her Maker, listening to Jesus' words: "I go away to prepare a place for you that where I am, you may also be."

Harriet was buried with full military honors at the base of a pine tree in Auburn, New York. Parks and museums mark her birthplace in Maryland and her final home in New York. A battleship was named in her honor, and postage stamps have been printed with her portrait. In 1990, March 10 was officially named "Harriet Tubman Day." Dozens of books have been written about her life. But the best memorial of all is how many people remember Harriet Tubman's fighting words: To reach any goal, put trust in your God and just "keep goin'."